THE HOUSE OF INVISIBLE BONDAGE

The Complete Cases of The Mongoose

BY JOHNSTON MCCULLEY

The Girl and the People of the Golden Atom

BY RAY CUMMINGS

*The Gray Dragon: The Adventures
of Peter the Brazen, Volume 2*

BY LORING BRENT

The Golden City

BY RALPH MILNE FARLEY

*The Scrap of Lace: The Complete Cases
of Madame Storey, Volume 1*

BY HULBERT FOOTNER

*Tower of Death: The Adventures of
Scarlet and Bradshaw, Volume 3*

BY THEODORE ROSCOE

The Devil-Tree of El Dorado

BY FRANK AUBREY

*The Firebrand: The Complete
Adventures of Tizzo, Volume 1*

BY MAX BRAND

*Marching Sands and The Caravan of the
Dead: The Harold Lamb Omnibus*

BY HAROLD LAMB

THE HOUSE OF INVISIBLE BONDAGE

THE COMPLETE CABALISTIC CASES OF SEMI DUAL, THE OCCULT DETECTOR

J.U. GIESY & JUNIUS B. SMITH

ILLUSTRATED BY

ROGER B. MORRISON

STEEGER BOOKS • 2019

PUBLISHING HISTORY

"The House of Invisible Bondage" originally appeared in the September 18, 25, October 2, and
9, 1926 issues of *Argosy All-Story Weekly* magazine (Vol. 180, No. 4–Vol. 181, No. 1).
Copyright © 1926 by The Frank A. Munsey Company. Copyright renewed © 1953 and
assigned to Steeger Properties, LLC. All rights reserved.

"About the Author: Dr. J.U. Giesy" originally appeared in the February 14, 1931 issue of *Argosy*
magazine (Vol. 218, No. 6). Copyright © 1931 by The Frank A. Munsey Company.
Copyright renewed © 1958 and assigned to Steeger Properties, LLC. All rights reserved.

"About the Author: Junius B. Smith" originally appeared in the February 21, 1931 issue of
Argosy magazine (Vol. 219, No. 1). Copyright © 1931 by The Frank A. Munsey Company.
Copyright renewed © 1958 and assigned to Steeger Properties, LLC. All rights reserved.

Visit steegerbooks.com for more books like this.

TABLE OF CONTENTS

The House of Invisible Bondage 1

About the Author: Dr. J.U. Giesy 178

About the Author: Junius B. Smith 180

CHAPTER I

DANGER BECKONS

"YOU CAN'T ALWAYS tell what a thing is by how it looks," said Bryce.

I nodded. We had been talking over cases we had handled, that morning in our suite of offices on the seventh floor of the Urania Building, indulging in reminiscence—as much as anything.

Jim was my partner in "Glace and Bryce—Private Investigators," and had been an inspector of police before our partnership was formed. He was a big-boned, heavy-set chap with a round head and a stubby brown mustache above the long, black cigar he was smoking. And he was a most dependable man.

He had come into my private room some half-hour before from his own on the other side of our suite, with a morning paper doubled up in his hand.

"Mornin', Gordon," he said, sitting down. "Well, here's another social luminary turned into a comet, started chasin' his tail an' gone clean out of his orbit."

"Yes?" I accepted his statement, which, though phrased in sidereal terms, was not at all enlightening to my mind. I had not read the paper carefully that morning, and, as a matter, of fact, Jim generally scanned the news more carefully than I.

"Yep!" He nodded, and shifted his cigar from one side of his mouth to the other. "Here's this Johnny, Imer Lamb, actin' a dammed sight more like a ram from all accounts—"

"Imer Lamb, the amateur tennis expert, golfer, swimmer, and

1

general all-around, athlete—the society Johnny who took up aviation recently? What's he done—crashed his plane?" I asked.

Jim grinned. "Not exactly his plane," he said. "But he's crashed all right. He's crashed his way into jail, accordin' to the paper. Beat up his valet over here in Monk's Hall, that bachelor apartment on Park Drive—almost killed him from all accounts—an' is taken to the hoosegow. Now what would a man want to beat up his valet for?"

"Well," I said, "I can think of any number of reasons from mere incompetency to meddling with his private stock." Actually, though, I felt my interest quicken to some extent.

Imer Lamb was a young man of exceedingly good looks and exceedingly plenteous means, who, since his father's death some years before, had cut a pretty wide swath in the social and sporting world. He had just missed the amateur tennis championship the previous year, and was equally good at golf. He had raced his speed car in Florida, and had recently taken to the air in the latest type of rich man's plaything-aeroplane that Hispano built. "Hasn't he a brother in the brokerage business?" I added.

"Sure," Jim agreed. "For that matter, he's in it himself. But he lets George do the work. He works at playing so far as I know anything about it. But the firm name's 'Lamb & Lamb.' Hot name for a firm of brokers. Accordin' to Hoyle, it oughta be Wolf Wolf."

"This assault on the valet occurred in Monk's Hall. That's where Dorien lived, remember?" I said, smiling at his words.

The remark led to a revamping not only of the case in which the man I had named had been a principal actor, but to others, each illustrative of the bent of the criminal mind, the battle of wits between those who sought to detect his identity, lay him by the heels, such as Jim and I, and the criminal himself. And that led to Jim's remark anent the fallacy of accepting the appearance of some incident at face value.

"Quite right. Then there was the Marya Townsend affair." Marya Townsend—her picture swam before my mental vision

as I spoke, dark-haired as some Oriental beauty with a hint of the Orient in her long-lashed, long-lidded, dark eyes; rich man's daughter, orphan who had been involved in a murder mystery that had cost an old man, her guardian, his life.

Bryce and I had been to some extent instrumental in straightening out the circumstantial tangle in which she was caught, thereby saving the budding romance of her life from being blasted at the start.

Jim chuckled as I spoke. "Well, yes," he said. "I ain't denyin', son, that you're right. That case was a swell collection of cross clues from beginnin' to end. But what's th' notion of draggin' Marya in again? That's about the third time you've mentioned Mrs. Harding, nee Townsend, this mornin'."

I laughed. As a matter of fact, he was right. I had referred to the wife of Bob Harding once or twice in the course of our conversation. So I looked him full in the eye. "To tell the truth, I've been thinking of her all morning, Jim," I said. "I don't know why I should be. As far as I know, I haven't thought of Marya for months. But she's crept into my consciousness this morning, and, womanlike, she refuses to be put out. Ever experience anything of the sort?"

"Oh, yes." He nodded, and grinned. "I reckon most everybody's done that at times. Only quite frequently, the parties what insinuated themselves into my mind wasn't such pleasant visitors as the little lady under discussion. Maybe she's payin' you the compliment of thinkin' of you, an' you're sort of feelin' it, son."

"A sort of unconscious telepathy?" I suggested.

"Somethin' of that sort." He nodded again. "She's thinkin' about you, say, an' you feel it without bein' able to interpret her thought-waves into any definite meanin', not bein' a Semi Dual, yourself."

Instinctively, I glanced at the little black box of a private telephone line on the wall of my room. It led up thirteen stories to the roof of the Urania, where the man, whose name he had uttered, lived.

Semi Dual! He was our friend. It was on his advice that Bryce and I had formed our partnership. Semi Dual, modern metaphysician, student of the higher life forces, those subtler unseen, often unsensed forces that regulate the very balance of the universe.

No charlatan, even though astrology, that older sister of astronomy, known to the ancients, in itself a manifestation of the interplay, of planetary electromagnetic energy by which the sweep of the universe is charted; telepathy, the thing Bryce had named, the conscious or unconscious perception of the inter-play of thought-waves generated in human brains; psychometry, the subjective, one might almost say spiritual, recognition of the well-nigh imperceptible vibratory emanations of an object, and their translation into definite meaning—were things he recognized as refractions of universal force through different media; and used.

For Semi Dual held all force to be one. The sweep of the seasons, the fury of elemental storms, the calm beauty of a June day, or the life we mortals possess, were to him but one and the same thing, manifested each in its proper time and place.

Semi Dual then, priest of justice, since to him justice, too, was no more than the working out of the law of cause and effect, a practical demonstration of the old, old declaration, that as a man soweth, so also shall he reap, measure for measure.

Such was our friend's creed. Under it, each man's action became no more than a seed from which good or evil, joy or sorrow, might be raised, according as to whether good or evil were embodied in the deed. The act was the seed, and the result the fruit. It was the only justice in which he believed.

High up in the tower above Bryce and me, as we sat that morning, he had taken up his abode in the midst of a garden of little walks between beds of blooming shrubs and flowers, ringed in by the vine-clad walls of the parapet of the roof.

There was even a little fountain and a sun-dial, beside the central path that led from the top of a bronze-and-marble stairway, mounting from the twentieth floor of the building to the tower, white and classic in its outlines, in which he dwelt.

In winter, the garden was roofed with sheltering plates of green-yellow glass. And at the head of the stairs let into the central pathway, was an annunciator plate of inlaid metal and glass, bearing a cryptic motto. Being trod upon it rang a chime of bells in the tower to herald a visitor's approach.

More than Bryce and I, Semi Dual, student of the occult— occult because not generally understood—forces of life, had been instrumental in freeing Marya Townsend from the circumstantial web in which she had been caught, in preserving her young life's happiness.

Literally he stood in the position of a god in the machine to me and Bryce. Having advised us to enter the field of private investigation, he had never withheld his help in any matter wherein he felt that his intervention was justified. Despite any hasty assumption which might evolve in the average mind from his manner of living, and the nature of his research, he was as practical as any man in his application of his knowledge, and far more consistent than most.

With his insight into life, its purposes, its impulses, and emotions, he could scarcely be anything else. Yet he held material things of little moment, and unless some problem in which we asked his aid involved what he termed "spiritual values"—the integrity of life or reputation, or the avenging of their loss—it failed to enlist his interest.

Tall, splendidly proportioned, with brown hair and carefully barbered Vandyke beard, deep gray eyes, an aquiline nose, and a head almost leonine in its suggestion, strong as a lion in defense of the right, of innocence, and virtue, sensitive as a woman in his every deeper feeling; such was the man whose mental image was evoked in my brain by my partner's words.

"Well, if Marya is thinking of me, I suppose I ought to feel honored in the fact alone," I said.

"Sure," Jim agreed without apparently considering that it was a bit unusual for a man who devoted his time to the unveiling of human crookedness to expose his more intimate feelings. "Any man ought to feel honored when a good woman takes him into her thoughts. The right sort of woman is about the finest thing what Dual calls the 'Cosmos' has evolved to date." He paused for the barest instant, and then added: "An' the other sort are hell, all right."

I smiled. While he was on the force Jim had been a "straight bull." He had every respect for a good woman as his last remark would indicate, and small use for one who was not.

He chuckled again. "Still I don't know why I should kick. They're the sort have been mixin' things up ever since the original pippin was harvested, an' one way an' another, they've furnished guys like us a lot of work. 'Churchy law fam' as the Frenchman says.

"The Frogs are right. Scratch a Russian, and you'll find a Tartar. Dig into almost any bit of human foolishness, an' you'll find a woman down at the bottom of it."

"You said a trunkful, old man. Go on; express yourself," I told him.

He shook his head. "No. I reckon I'll cancel the chant, now I've got that off my chest. Referrin' to our lamb chops, however, an' assumin' that Marya really is thinkin' of you, it would be interestin' if you was better able to tune in on her thoughts."

"Are you trying to intimate that it is strange she should devote them to me?" I suggested.

"Admittin' that without argument," he retorted, " I am not. It isn't why, but what she's thinkin', I'm askin' myself. I'd sort of hate to think she'd run up against Major Trouble again. Anything of that sort."

His words gave me pause. I had not thought of that possible angle to the matter. "What sort of trouble?" I asked.

"I don't know, of course." Jim once more rolled his deadly-looking cigar across his mouth. "But she was in trouble enough the first time she met us, an' it would be natural for her to think of us now in case she had bumped into some unpleasantness again. That's why I said it would be interestin' to be able to get her wave length."

"See here, Jim; are you serious?" I said. Up to that minute I had regarded our entire discussion as more or less hypothetical.

"Of course I'm serious," he grumbled. "She wouldn't be thinking of you unless there was a reason why she should."

I grinned at him. "Suppose she's not thinking of me at all. Suppose I'm just thinking of her instead."

"Why?" he demanded shortly, staring me straight in the face.

"Why what?" I countered.

"Why should you be thinkin' of her? Why should you come up here this mornin' an' start thinkin' of another man's wife?" he said.

His attitude surprised me. It seemed to me that he was making far more out of the situation than it deserved. "Naturally I don't know, and I can't see that it matters," I told him.

He refused to be sidetracked. "But it does," he declared. "It matters just this much, that in sayin' just what you have, you've proved my point. You're thinkin' of her without knowin' why. Therefore, you're thinkin' of her because she's thinkin' of you, an' you get her thought to that extent.

"Things don't happen without a cause. If Marya Harding is

thinkin' of you hard enough to drive the impression into that armored turret of yours, she must have a good reason."

Behind me—across from Jim as we sat— sharply staccato in its sound, the little telephone box on the wall emitted a buzz.

It cut into Jim's words; it cut them off. It left him sitting there, staring, with jaw half-sagged, at the box out of which it whirred.

As for myself, it brought me half out of my chair with every nerve tensing to sudden attention. As I have said, it was the lower end of the private wire to the quarters of Semi Dual. And it never rang unless there was some very definite reason, some very urgent need.

I went toward it, and removed the receiver from the hook. "Yes. Glace speaking," I answered its demand.

"Good morning, Gordon," Semi Dual's voice returned along the wire. "If Mrs. Robert Harding, who was Miss Marya Townsend, should come to you with a request affecting me in any way whatsoever, bring her, together with any one who may accompany her, to me."

"Very well," I said, and hung up. I was not very much surprised. Amazing as the thing might appear from any ordinary viewpoint to the uninitiated, I had, even as Jim, who still sat behind me waiting, had pointed out, known Semi Dual to give more than one similar demonstration of the uncanny ability he possessed before.

I simply turned around and told him what Dual had directed me to do, and watched his jaws tighten on the cigar between their teeth.

"An' that does prove it, son," he rumbled in a tone of conviction. "She was thinkin' of him as well as us, I reckon, an' he knew how to get her wave-length. That's all there is to it, of course. I guess it proves that Marya's, in need of help of some sort."

I nodded.

"Semi said she'd have somebody with her?" he suggested.

"He intimated as much," I said.

"Huh," he grunted, and lapsed silent.

I said nothing more. There seemed nothing more to be said under the conditions. Apparently Jim was right; Bob Harding's wife had been forcibly turning her thoughts in our direction, unconsciously projecting them from herself to us. And they had reached us. Only Semi Dual had been able to not only feel but read them, while I had no more than sensed their tiny fingers beating against my brain.

Jim and I sat there until, after possibly half an hour, Nellie Newel, our chief clerk, rapped on the door of my room and came in, bringing with her a card.

"Mrs. Robert Harding is outside, Mr. Glace, with another young woman. She wants to see you, if possible," she announced.

I reached for the card and took it, and handed it to Bryce.

"Very well, Nellie," I said. "Show Mrs. Harding and her companion in at once."

CHAPTER II

TO THE CRIME WIZARD

MISS NEWELL WITHDREW, closing the door behind her. Jim and I looked into one another's eyes. Semi Dual had demonstrated the subtle, qualities that made it hard indeed to take him unawares. Something more than a half-hour ago he had indicated the belief that Marya Harding would call upon us with a companion. She was here—would appear before us inside a minute.

"Well," said Jim, laying his cigar on an ashtray upon my desk in expectation of her entrance, "that's that. Now, what the devil—"

The door swung open. Marya Harding came through it smiling, together with a somewhat younger woman who did not smile.

My major attention centered on the second woman. Marya was beautiful, as always, in that dark, Oriental fashion of hers; but this second girl was like a beam of sunshine half dimmed by an intervening cloud.

She was slender and blond, with hair the color of strained honey, eyes of an almost pansy purple, and lips a trifle set now as though by the stress of inner emotion, but which one fancied could be tender on occasion, beneath a straight patrician little nose. Oh, yes, there was breeding in that face, the lines and angles that spoke of past generations of careful selection in blood. And not only in her face but in her bearing, as Marya made the introductions, were those past generations displayed.

One felt it, knew that Moira Mason was a beautiful creation it had taken a long time to produce, the fruit of a family tree that had been long in growth.

And of course I knew who she was. Heaven knew her name was often enough in the papers, her picture on the society page. Moira Mason was the daughter of Adrian Mason, one of our city's most aggressive and influential financiers.

Bryce nodded his head in recognition.

"Miss Mason," I said, and took the slim hand she extended briefly into my own, and found its fingers cold.

We gave our visitors chairs. Marya sank into hers, still smiling. Marriage, I thought, had improved her. She had never seemed more charming to me before. But still I knew, even as she settled herself gracefully in her seat, that our interest was not with her—that it lay in Moira Mason, the clouded sunbeam of a woman whom until that moment I had thought of, if at all, as a human butterfly.

And Marya's first words after she was seated confirmed my evaluation of the situation. She came directly to the reason for their call, though in a fashion that showed a slight embarrassment.

"I hope you gentlemen won't think I'm forming a habit of running to you every time I'm in need of help, but will just feel that whenever there is a need you are the men I think of first. Really, though, it's Moira who needs the sort of assistance you can render.

"And I told her I was positive you would give it. I made her come, promised her to explain, and see if we could enlist your aid. I told her all you and your wonderful friend Mr. Semi Dual had done for Bob and me in the past. I—I—thought—felt sure—from what I know of him—that if you would intercede for us—he might be willing to help her, if anything can be done. You see, she was engaged to Mr. Imer Lamb, and—"

"Imer Lamb!" Jim exploded.

I couldn't blame him either. Imer Lamb was in jail for an

assault upon his valet, if one could believe the newspaper account Jim had quoted to me this morning. Here was a beautiful girl, his fiancée, her features shadowed by trouble, appealing to us through a mutual friend, in Imer Lamb's behalf. I glanced at her, and back to Marya Harding.

She was looking straight at Jim.

"You know, then, about his arrest," she was saying. "That's bad enough, of course. But there is more to it than the papers print. It's—that I hoped to take up with Mr. Dual, if we could induce you to sponsor our request. His—attack on his valet is really only the culmination of something that has been going on for some time. If we could see your friend—explain—"

I interrupted. "We understand fully, Mrs. Harding, and there will be no difficulty in what you ask. You know Semi Dual, and you know something of the way in which he works. Because of that I am going to tell you now that your request was granted before ever you made it in words. Before you reached here this morning Dual called us on the telephone and instructed us to bring you and Miss Mason to him as soon as you arrived."

Her eyes widened.

"He called you—told you that?" she exclaimed softly and glanced at Moira Mason, who had lifted herself to a tensely erect position on her chair.

"Just that," I told her. "Of course he did not mention Miss Mason's name, but he spoke of your bringing a companion."

"But," she began, "we spoke of coming here to no one. How—"

"Did he know?" I interrupted again. "You thought about it, talked it over between yourselves; and he caught your thought, Mrs. Harding, and read your intent. It is telepathy—a sort of mental radio, if you like. He does that sort of thing."

"It's wonderful, almost unbelievable," she said. "Do you hear, Moira? He's going to see us; and he'll help Imer. I feel sure he will."

"It is—wonderful indeed," Moira Mason spoke for the first time since she had been seated.

"Then, can we go to him now?" Marya Harding prompted.

"Of course," I agreed, and rose.

Five minutes later I escorted both women from the elevator grille on the twentieth floor to the bronze and marble stairway that led to Semi Dual's domain on the roof.

We mounted. It was a July day, and Semi's garden, slumbered under the light of late morning like a dream picture more than a scene of the modern world. There were beds of shrubbery and flowers flanking the central path, the nodding, drowsy heads roses, red and white and yellow. Their perfume was a warm spice in our nostrils.

And before us was the tower, a thing of dark etched shadows, and whiteness. There was the tiny fountain with a gray and white dove on the rim of its basin, and the little ancient sundial marking the hour of our approach.

Moira Mason cried out softly as we reached the top.

At the sound of her soft-toned exclamation, I glanced at the girl. Surprised admiration was in her face.

I trod on the annunciator plate. The chimes in the tower rang mellow as the distant note of an old-time shepherd's pipe. Other doves rose up from its facade and fluttered into startled flight.

Marya Harding spoke with a little catch in, her words. "But, Mr. Glace, this is marvelous—like a picture come to life."

"It is the place Dual has made to insure himself quiet, while he studies life," I said, and led the way up the central path to the door of the tower, etched a dark oblong in its nearer side.

It stood open before us, and, as we entered, Henri—Dual's one companion in the seclusion he customarily maintained, bowed before us, a tray in his hands.

On it were three glasses of a sparkling beverage I recognized as a blend of pure fruit juices, wonderfully refreshing, which I had tasted more than once.

"Welcome, *mesdames* and *monsieur*," Henri greeted our arrival. "The master requests that you drink, and refresh yourselves."

We stood in the anteroom to Semi's quarters, an apartment

done in varying shades of brown. I myself handed their glasses to the two women, and noted their glance run about the room.

"This is like the 'Arabian Nights,'" Marya. Harding laughed in a somewhat nervous fashion, and sipped at her glass.

I smiled at her. It was all an old story to me. But I could quite appreciate its effect on those who came upon it without warning. It had impressed me in somewhat the same fashion the first time, and since. I drained my glass, took hers and Moira Mason's from their hands, replaced them on Henri's tray.

He deposited the latter on a little table.

"And now the master awaits the ladies' pleasure," he said. "You know the way, M. Glace."

I nodded. There was a door on the farther side that gave into a room beyond. I crossed to it and rapped.

"Enter."

I set the door open and ushered my companions through it.

Dual sat at a huge desk, clad, as was his custom when at home, in a flowing robe of white, edged with purple on cuff and collar. Beyond him a window, its expanse occupying nearly the whole width of the room, threw his splendid head into silhouette. Beyond him also; at one end of the desk, a life-sized bronze figure of Venus, really an electrolier, held an apple of golden glass in a gracefully outstretched hand. There was a great clock in a corner, a wonderful Persian rug upon the floor.

I closed the door behind me.

Semi Dual rose. Bending from the hips, he bowed. Before straightening he smiled.

"Welcome, Marya, the fingers of whose soul I have felt seeking contact with mine this morning," he said. "And thou"—he turned his glance to Moira Mason, his gray eyes searching her face—"whom I perceive to be troubled in spirit, so that I deem that thy sister woman brings thee to me in thy, rather than her own, behalf, thou art welcome also."

"Thank you," Miss Mason said in little more than a whisper. One could see her visibly affected by Semi Dual's costume and manner as well as his speech and his instant appraisal of the situation as affecting her.

Marya, however, was in a measure prepared for something of the sort from her contact with him in the past. She presented Moira by name, and we all found seats.

"And now tell me," Semi prompted, once more with a smile upon his lips.

It was Marya who complied, at first. Briefly she told him what she had already told Bryce and me. Semi Dual watched her closely.

"Moira came to me this morning after she knew of his arrest," she said. "I thought that if you would listen to her story you might be able to tell her how it would all come out."

"At least I shall listen," Dual spoke after a momentary silence that followed her words. "It is written, 'Seek and ye shall find, knock and it shall be opened unto you, ask and ye shall receive.' Wherefore I shall listen, and if it lie within my power I shall give."

His gray eyes turned again to Moira Mason. "Tell me, my child."

"There is so little to tell," she said, almost like a puzzled child indeed. "I really don't understand. It's like a nightmare. Imer is so different from what he was. It's as though some evil power had changed him lately—since we have been engaged. I've known him a long time, and—a—a dearer boy never lived.

"But in the last month he hasn't been himself; he's been irritable, irascible. And I'd never known him to lose control of himself before. We quarreled a few days ago. You know he's been flying of late. He's been doing stunt flying. It's very dangerous. I asked him to be careful, and he flew into a rage, became actually violent. I tried to calm him, tried to put my arms about his neck, and he tore them away and threw me from him, and rushed out of the house. See—" She extended an arm on which were the discolored marks of fingers.

"And before that he'd always been gentle, for all his strength.

He's a strong man, Mr. Dual. I'm sure he wouldn't have willingly hurt me. Yet he did. And yet the very next day he came back as though nothing had happened.

"He didn't mention it. It was as though he didn't know, or had forgotten. And now—last night—he attacked his valet, beating him, choking him, apparently meaning to kill him. They say he would have killed him if a neighbor had not heard the noise of their fight and rushed in and helped his man overpower Imer until they could call the police. It—it almost seems as though he were going—crazy."

She broke off with a caught-in breath and quivering lips.

Dual stirred, opened his eyes, sat up. While she had been speaking he had been lying back in his chair relaxed. One might have fancied from his posture, his closed eyes, the slow rise and fall of his chest, that he slept. But I, who knew him, knew also that he did not; that back of his lowered lids his alert mind was doubly awake, was focusing, centering all its analytical ability on her words, apprehending her every slightest statement, apprais-ing it, marking it for a future reference perhaps.

"You love him?" he said now.

"Oh, yes."

Faint color stole into Moira Mason's cheeks.

"And how well do you love him?" Semi Dual demanded.

"Why, I, hardly know how to answer," she faltered. "How does one put a value on—love?"

Semi Dual nodded. "How indeed?" he returned. "But let me put it this way. Do you love him more than yourself?"

"Oh, yes." She did not hesitate.

"Then," Semi said, "answer me such questions as I shall ask. You have known him a long time. Do you know of any past worries, any unpleasant episodes in his life?"

"No-o." She shook her head. "He's always seemed more a happy, care-free boy to me than anything else."

"He has not been prone to dissipation?" he asked.

"Not any real dissipation," she said.

"Does he drink? Have you ever seen him intoxicated?"

"No—never. He takes an occasional drink, but not enough to muddle him ever. He smokes a good deal. No, Mr. Dual, he is not a dipsomaniac."

Dual turned to me with a question. "Do you know anything of the young man in question, Gordon?"

I told, him briefly what Jim had told: me that morning concerning Lamb's connection with the brokerage firm operated by his brother.

"But George isn't really his brother," Moira amended my information when I had ceased. "He is no relation really, except by adoption. He is really the son of a friend of Imer's father. When the man died and left George an orphan, after asking Imer's father to take care of his child, Mr. Lamb adopted him."

Semi Dual turned to his desk, took a sheet of paper from a neatly piled stack upon it, and picked up a pencil.

"And what is Imer's age?" he asked. "Give me as nearly as possible the day, month, and hour of his birth, as well as the place."

"He was born right here," Moira told him. "And he'll be twenty-seven on the 29th of this coming September. I know that, but I do not know the hour. Is it important?"

"If he was born here we can possibly gain the information from the vital statistics of the Board of Health," Semi said. "And now the same information concerning yourself if you please."

She complied. I saw her delicately chiseled nostrils flare. "You're going to work, aren't you?" she cried as Semi wrote down the data she furnished. "Marya told me something about how you do it. You're going to tell me if anything can be done for Imer—how everything is going to turn out?"

"Perhaps." Dual finished jotting down the' information he had asked for. "Do you know at what time he attacked his valet last night?"

"It was somewhere around midnight," Miss Mason replied.

"At least George says so. I saw him this morning. He was trying to get Imer released on bail, but so far without success."

"The police blotter will show the time of the arrest at least," Dual said. "You saw your friend, Mr. Imer Lamb, this morning?"

For a moment the girl's lips quivered again before she answered. "Oh, yes, I went to the jail, but he didn't seem to want to talk. He told me to stay away in the future."

"You say he did not wish to talk?" Semi questioned. "Just how did he appear, Miss Mason?"

"He seemed depressed—morose," Moira explained. "He asked me to have George bring him a pipe and some tobacco, and I said I would. And I called George after I left Imer. That was when he told me he was trying to arrange for his release on bail."

"The valet was seriously injured?" Semi queried.

"No." She shook her head. "Fortunately not. Mr. Lamb said he wasn't going to make any trouble for Imer, and that he had asked to stay on at Imer's apartment until he can arrange to get him out. But if Imer is really going insane—" Once more her voice broke.

"Peace," said Semi Dual, reverting from the more modern beating and diction which had held him during the last few minutes to that he had employed at first. "Peace, thou troubled child! What shall be, time and time only will tell. Yet I have listened to you, and now I shall seek to do whatsoever I can.

"And there are certain steps to be taken before I may learn what I shall learn. Therefore abide in peace, and strengthen thy heart with this thought, that all things pass, even as clouds from off the sun. That which today is a riddle, tomorrow we shall understand.

"Wherefore today I shall seek to read the riddle you have placed before me. And tomorrow I shall strive to place at least a portion of the truth within your hands. Take that thought with thee in leaving me to the task which is now become mine."

The interview was ended. He rose. Marya, and Moira Mason,

and I regained our feet. Semi bowed to the women, touched their hands.

"Peace," he said again to Moira. "It is the greatest boon, my child. Hence we use the word in parting from a friend. Peace with thee till tomorrow." Again he bowed.

Once we were back in the garden passing toward the stairway from it to the busy twentieth century world, she spoke, addressing me directly:

"Your friend is a strange man, Mr. Glace—a strange man."

CHAPTER III

VIEWING THE PRISONER

I COULD FANCY how Semi Dual in his garden, his robes of white and purple, must have impressed her. I knew because since I had known him, time and again he had impressed me, myself. A strange man indeed.

And never before or since I think did his course impress me as more strange than in the days that followed him first meeting with Moira Mason, days wherein the real meaning; the real purpose back of his move was deeply hidden from Jim and me as the strange, and to us unimagined condition, they were deliberately planned to oppose.

After they left I went into my private room at our offices. I was puzzled. Viewed from an ordinary viewpoint, there was little in the affair that had brought Marya Harding and her girl friend to the interview just closed. On its face it was no more than the mental distress of a woman over a change in the personality of the man to whom she was engaged.

From her side of the matter that was enough. But if Imer Lamb, rich man's son, sportsman, dilettante, had developed a latent strain of insanity within the past few weeks, I couldn't see where even Semi Dual would be able, to help.

However, I was not left long to myself, Jim came thrusting his way in along a little corridor that ran from his room to mine across the back of our suite.

"Well?" he demanded sinking into a chair, his brown eyes searching my face.

"I don't know, Jim," I confessed, and told him what had occurred.

"Meanin' Lamb's goin' cuckoo?" he said frowning. "Then what in time does Semi hope to accomplish beyond transferrin' him from jail to the psychopathic ward?"

"Naturally, I don't know that either. I don't believe Dual does as yet," I said. "Presumably, however, he may have an idea that a study of Lamb's horoscope will show indications as to whether his present condition is temporary or not."

"Well, yes." Jim nodded still frowning. "An', of course, he made the girl give him at least part of the dope he needed to set up one of those astrological charts of his. But if this valet isn't goin' to press charges against his Employer I wonder what the hitch is in arranging bail."

"Isn't it just possible that your suggestion about transferring Lamb to the psychopathic ward may apply to that?" I offered an explanation. "Possibly they suspect that they actually have a psychopathic case."

"Huh!" Jim grunted in comprehension and pursed his upper lip, bristling his stubby brown mustache. "Well, I hadn't thought of that till now, but if one of the city docs has seen him, it might work out like that. An', of course, if they did, they'd hold him till they was sure whether it was safe to turn him out or not. I've half a mind to drift down an' have a chin with Johnson, an' see what he says."

Inspector Johnson had been Jim's pal when he was still, "on the force." And Bryce had formed the habit of dropping in at the station for a chat at such times as we were not pressed by work. So now it occurred to me that by following his suggestion he might at least obtain the police side of the matter provided Johnson was inclined to talk.

"Go ahead!" I assented. "You can't do any harm and you may be able to find out just what sort of a disturbance of the peace Lamb really pulled. From what Miss Mason told upstairs this morning, it wasn't lamblike in the least."

Jim grinned. "All right. I'll mosey down there," he said, then paused as, for the second time, the private telephone buzzed. "I'll wait till you answer that first."

I was on my feet already as he spoke. For the second time I unhooked the receiver and spoke into the transmitter.

"Yes, this is Glace."

And then I stood and listened while the man on the roof voiced his directions very much as a general might speak to a lieutenant in the field, briefly, concisely, without any circumlocution or explanation as to why they were issued, beyond the tacit assumption that each encompassed an action required.

"Very well," I assented to them at the end of possibly a minute, replaced the receiver, and turned back to Bryce.

"As a matter of fact, we're both going over to the station," I said. "And after that we're going to see this valet of Lamb's, and if possible that foster brother of his besides."

"He told you to do that?" As he spoke Bryce jerked his head toward the ceiling.

"All of it," I told him, and reached for my hat.

"Just what did he tell you?" Jim demanded.

"He told me," I said, "to go to the jail, Monk's Hall, and to see George Lamb, and learn anything we could. Come along."

We left the office, descended to the street, and arrived at the Central Station in due time. Bryce smoked most of the way in silence. As a matter of fact, neither of us was really very clear in his mind as to just what we were going to do.

Finally Jim put some of that uncertainty into words. "My original notion was just to run over here and see Johnson. But now what? Are we supposed to try and see Lamb?"

And I considered that point for a few steps before I answered: "I've an idea, Jim, that the best thing is to follow out your original plan. We'll find Johnson, and sort of let the conversation that follows shape our actions. As a matter of fact, from all ordinary standards we've no particular call to feel any particular interest in Lamb."

"Uh-huh." He nodded as we mounted the steps of the station. "Just sort of stall along and watch for the breaks, eh? All right, son."

"Johnson about?" He spoke to the sergeant on the desk as we entered.

"Sure. In the 'tecs room. Mornin', Jim. How are you, Mr. Glace?" Sergeant Harrington returned.

He was a man grown gray in the service; we had both known him a long time.

"Fine, Dan," I said, and followed Bryce toward the door of the detectives' room on the far side of the front office.

Bryce threw it open without the ceremony of a rap, and we both went in.

Inspector Johnson, large, heavily built, with a rather florid face, always the rough and ready type of officer; glanced up from the desk where he was sitting.

"Hello!" he said. "What is it—a general alarm?"

Bryce grinned, and helped himself to a chair. I followed suit.

"Nope," Jim made answer, sitting down, "it is just one way of wasting time, I guess."

Johnson eyed him. Usually they indulged in a similar sort of repartee when together.

"Wastin' mine, or yours?" he suggested.

"Both," Jim countered, "unless you've got somethin' on hand requirin' help."

That was a dig, since more than once Johnson, in his official capacity, had appealed to both Glace Bryce, and even Semi Dual, for aid, and had received what he asked.

And seemingly he sensed more than a mere retort back of my partner's response. His eyelids tensed a trifle, he dropped his air of persiflage, and became incisively direct.

"What's up, Jim?" he asked.

"Imer Lamb," Bryce answered him in two words.

"Huh! That bird?" Johnson stared.

"Yep!" I nodded. "I understand you caged him last night on a probable charge of assault with intent to kill. Just how many sorts of hell did he raise?"

"He raised enough, from all accounts, while it lasted," Johnson said slowly. "Tried to choke the life out of his man, a chap by the name of Joe Kingsley, an' bash in his dome with the butt of an automatic, before another Johnny over in Monk's Hall heard the rough-house an' broke in an' dragged him off."

"Had a gun, eh?" Jim said, verbally noting the point as Johnson paused.

"Yep—regular army pattern," the inspector assented.

"Moonshine?" Bryce suggested; and I knew he was merely seeking to learn what Johnson thought.

But his denial was instant. "Nope! From what we know, Lamb's not a hoochhound, even if he is a high roller."

"Bad blood between him an' Kingsley? Jim suggested.

"Hardly, I think. The fellow isn't even goin' to press a charge. What do you want to know for?" Johnson demanded.

"Just givin' you credit for havin' given the arrest of a man in Lamb's position some consideration," Bryce told him, grinning. "But—I guess it's not important. If Kingsley don't appear against him, you'll have to spring him."

Johnson took his time before he answered. One might have thought he was trying to decide how far to accept Jim's reply at its face.

"I don't know about that," he said at length. "Listen! You two come clean as to why you want the low-down on this bozo, an' I'll spill you something. Now kick in."

"Looks like we'd have to, don't it, Gordon?" Bryce glanced at me with another grin. "First, though, I'd like to know when Lamb was arrested. If I knew that—"

"The call came into the Park Drive Station at twelve twenty-five this morning;" Johnson interrupted. "Now, what's if all about?"

We told him, and he listened with a growing expression of

puzzlement on his face. Apparently Moira Alason's visit to Dual surprised him in no small degree, and at the same time coincided with certain phases of the matter within his knowledge as shown by his comment when our account was finished:

"Well, that all matches up. That's why I said I wasn't sure whether Lamb would be sprung or not. From all we could gather from his valet, Kingsley, the attack was totally unprovoked. According to him, Lamb had been sort of sullen all evening, had spent the evening at home, and just sat around and smoked.

"He went to bed about eleven, and somewhere after midnight Kingsley, who was just retiring, says he came into his room with the gun in his hand and hopped at him without a word, outside a funny sort of noise in his throat. That led us to havin' Dr. Simpson see him this morning early, an' Simpson's of the opinion that Lamb may be going off his nut. So he was engaged to old Adrian Mason's daughter, was he?"

Jim nodded. He was puffing out his stubby mustache. "An' it was Simpson's opinion that blocked his brother in gettin' him out this mornin'," he said. "You're holdin' him for observation?"

"We're goin' to hold him," Johnson agreed. "After last night Simpson says he thinks he's got hold of a case of homicidal mania, or something of the sort. An' of course if he's right, springing that sort of a gil is something he wouldn't stand for."

"Naturally not," I agreed.

Dr. Simpson was one of the leading members of the city medical service, and a man whose opinion could hardly fail to bear considerable weight. It was easy enough, therefore, to see why Lamb would in all probability continue in durance whether his valet saw fit to appear against him for the assault of the previous night, or not.

"I suppose at that rate you'll transfer him to the county observation ward?" I suggested.

"That's the way it looks now," Johnson replied. "But what I can't get is why Dual should have come into the thing, or why he should have shot you two down here to gather an earful as he has."

"Actually," I said, "I don't know that he really is in it as yet. As we told you, Miss Mason saw him this morning, and he told her he'd see what he learned by tomorrow. That's all we know ourselves. But of course if he should feel that Lamb is develop-ing a homicidal mania it goes almost without saying he would be the last man in the world to suggest that he be turned loose. What Miss Mason seemed to want to know as much as anything else was how the affair was coming out."

"Find out where she stood?" Johnson said. "Well, that's natu-ral enough. And from what I know of Dual, he ought to be able to tell her, if any one could. I've known him to call the turn on more than one thing before this."

"What's Lamb doing now?" Jim asked.

"He isn't doing anything," Johnson declared. "Just sitting in his cell, Simpson says. Says he lets on he don't know what it's all about. Want to see our playboy? If you do, I can take you back?"

"Sure. Let's see how he's takin' it now." Jim rose.

Johnson and I followed him up. Things were working out about to my liking just then. So far we had learned the approxi-mate time of Lamb's arrest, and the name of the valet we had yet to see at Monk's Hall, and the fact that Lamb had used the butt of an army model automatic on the latter's head. About all that was needed now to complete the success of our call on Johnson was to see the man himself.

"Still," Jim spoke again as we waited outside the jail grating, "I wouldn't call him a playboy, Johnson, I guess. If the war had gone on a little longer, a few years ago, Imer Lamb would have come home an American ace. As it was, he did quite a bit of flying over there before the show closed. Got shot down back of the German lines durin' an offensive, was knocked out an' left for dead, an' found after our boys carried their objective an' was mopin' up. Maybe he's been a playboy the last few years, but along in 1918 he was sure doin' a he-man's stuff."

"The devil he was!" Johnson's tone showed a quickened interest. "Well, see here. If that's right, maybe that's how come he had an army gat in his rooms last night. You're sure of that dope, are you, Bryce?"

"Dead sure. It was in the papers at the time, if you'd happened to read it," Jim reaffirmed.

"An' you always was a hog for readin'," Johnson nodded as a turnkey opened the gate.

We went back, along a corridor of cells, to one within which a younger man sat, elbows on his knees, head in hands, upon the edge of the cot.

As we paused outside the cell door he lifted his face. He was handsome. I admitted it after a first glance, handsome in a masculine way, with a perfect cast of features neither effeminate nor weak.

"Hello, Lamb!" Johnson accosted him. "Just what was your idea in tryin' to bean that man of yours last night?"

Lamb stared. For a long moment he held Johnson's glance. And then he frowned. "If I knew, I'd tell you I think, whoever you are. But I'm damned if I know a thing about it, old man," he said.

"Utterly lost your memory about that pettin' party you staged at your place, have you?" Johnson sneered.

And suddenly the beauty of Imer Lamb's face was marred. For just a moment a something hard, to define looked out of his eyes. They looked like those of an animal about to spring, but the expression passed.

"That won't get you anything, old chap," he said. "If I don't remember, I don't, do I? After you've answered that you can answer another question, too, if you like. Has that brother of mine been back here since early this morning? Asked him to get me some tobacco, and I'm dyin' for a smoke."

"I ain't seen him if he has," Johnson told him, abandoning any attempt toward getting him to talk of his attack on Kingsley. "Meet Mr. Glace and Mr. Bryce."

"Glad to meet you, gentlemen, whoever you are." Imer Lamb smiled faintly. "Always pleasant to make a new acquaintance. What is this, a tour of Who's Zoo, or what?"

"Well, not exactly," said Jim, reaching into a pocket. "Here, if you've got a yen for tobacco, have a smoke." He passed him one of his deadly-looking cigars through the cell door grating.

"Thanks." Lamb took it, and Jim struck a match, holding it so that the man in the cell might obtain a light.

Lamb bit off the tip with an eager motion of strong white teeth, and held the end to the flame, drawing deeply upon the weed, and exhaling a mouthful of smoke. Once, twice, three times he repeated the performance, and then he grimaced in a fashion of distaste, withdrew the cigar from his lips, and eyed it in evident disfavor.

"Too bad," he said.

Johnson grinned. I felt my own lips twitch. Bryce had a strong taste in tobacco.

"Too bad," Lamb repeated. "You'll pardon me, sir, since I assume your actions were kindly in intent, but that's a filthy bit of weed. Really, I couldn't smoke it. I've always said our police were paid too little by far."

Johnson snorted. Jim went red to the eyes. "Smoke it or throw it away, whichever suits you, brother," he growled. "It's good enough for me."

"Oh, but I meant no offense, you know," Lamb protested. "Tastes differ, you see. That's' life. My brother George and I smoke a blend made out of carefully aged and ripened leaves. George discovered it some months ago, got a chance to get it. It's not on the market. Private stock and all that. We've used it ever since."

"Go right on an' use it, son," Bryce told him. Plainly the episode had got a bit under his skin. He turned, and strolled up the corridor toward the end of the tier of cells. I glanced at Johnson and we followed, leaving Lamb looking after, gripping the grating of the cell door with a strong and well-formed hand.

Back outside I asked Johnson for the use of a telephone. It occurred to me that there was one bit of information now in our possession which Dual might find of use. I called him, using the private number unlisted but in my possession. And then Bryce and I made our way again to the street.

Jim pulled a cigar from his pocket, and lighted it on the station steps.

"Let that filthy thing alone," I began, unable to resist the impulse.

And he chuckled. "I wasn't sure when I came down here," he said as he fell into step beside me. "But I am now. Takin' all things into consideration, Imer Lamb's insane, all right."

CHAPTER IV

MONK'S HALL

I SUGGESTED LUNCH, and we stopped at a cafe before setting out for Monk's Hall, the fashionable bachelor apartment house on fashionable Park Drive.

It was a many-storied building with an ornate foyer, an office, a desk, and a uniformed elevator attendant in charge of a many-mirrored cage inside a grille of ornamental type.

Inquiry at the desk elicited the information that Kingsley was in Lamb's rooms. We had a request for an interview telephoned up.

"He wants to know who it is, sir?" the desk attendant said after a moment.

Bryce flung himself into the breach. "Tell him we are friends of Miss Mason," he said.

Kingsley asked that we be sent up.

"Suite 410," the youth at the switchboard told us, and we made our way to the waiting elevator cage.

Two minutes later we were rapping on the door of the indicated suite.

It was opened by Kingsley himself. At least I had little doubt that the man who opened to us was Kingsley, since to all appearances at least he might well have been the victim of an assault. There was a bandage about his throat, and another around his head. He was a medium-sized individual with thin hair, a face wearing an expression of pain, and a pair of china blue eyes, separated by a slightly twisted nose which looked as though it might have been broken and badly set in the past.

"Come hin, gentlemen," he invited, and I noted that as he closed the door behind us and followed us into a handsomely appointed living room off the tiny entrance hall, he walked with a limp amounting to almost an actual halt—a dragging of one leg, some injury of the past it struck me, rather than any recent hurt.

"Be seated, gentlemen." He gave us chairs. He was cockney English beyond a doubt. "Hif you're friends hof Miss Mason you're welcome. Hi presume Miss Mason his ha bit hupset hover wat 'appened lawst night. Rum go the marster, tryin' to do me in, w'at?"

"So that's the way you feel about it, is it?" Bryce said as Kingsley took our hats. "Well, you're right about Miss Mason. She's upset all right. They tell me you're going to pass it over, Kingsley, not going to press the charge against Lamb."

"Ho, but, sir, Hi couldn't do that." Kingsley's tone was one almost of shocked surprise. "The marster, bless 'im, didn't know w'at he was doin', hof course. 'E's a toff, sir—a toff hif ever there was. Treated me swell 'e has for years. Saved my life 'e did in eighteen, time Hi got my leg. You may 'ave noticed hit, sirs. Guv me my blighty, ho yus.

"But by then Hi didn't 'ave no 'ome to go to, hand Mr. Himer 'e says, 'Well, Joe, hi'll take care hof you,' 'e says. Hand 'e's done hit, sirs. Hi'm not good for much. But hi howe 'im ha lot. Too much to make 'im hany trouble hover lawst night. Ho, yus, much too much. Miss Mason didn't arsk you to call, account hof that, did she, sirs?"

"No, she didn't. Lamb's brother George had already told her you didn't mean to make trouble," I informed him. As a matter of fact, I was a good deal taken with Kingsley. Gratitude of his type is unusual enough to be noteworthy. And, of course, what he had told us about Lamb's having saved his life during the war was something of a surprise. Lamb seemed to have been a good deal of a man a few years ago, even as Bryce had told Johnson at the jail.

Kingsley nodded slightly as I paused. "Hi didn't think she would," he declared. "Ha fine little lady—a bit of arl right, sir, hif Hi may so hexpress myself."

The fellow was frankness itself.

"See here, Kingsley," I said. "Let's get things straight. Really, we're no more friends of Miss Mason than we are of Lamb's. We merely told the desk that in order to insure our getting up. This—" I glanced at Jim—"is Mr. James Bryce, and I am Mr. Gordon Glace. Miss Mason came to us through a mutual friend this morning in Mr. Lamb's behalf. Our errand really is to learn from you as nearly as you can tell it exactly what happened last night as well as to discover whether or not you have noticed any change in Mr. Lamb the past few weeks."

Kingsley's wits were decidedly quicker than his halting gait. "Gor blyme!" he exclaimed, turning his glance from me to Bryce. "Gor blyme, sirs; you're by way of bein' detectives then, I fawncy—somethin' of the sort."

"Private detectives, Kingsley," I told him. "We're not of the police. But you see, the police doctor thinks Mr. Lamb may be not quite himself—mentally that is."

"Balmy!" he interrupted. "You mean, sir, they think 'e's balmy? My word! Not but w'at 'is 'oppin' at me lawst night might seem a bit crazy, like for the time 'e was hoff 'is 'ead. Hi'm thinkin' hit was a nightmare myself, something hof the sort."

"Just a minute, Kingsley," I interrupted his protests. "Didn't you tell the police that Lamb had been acting sullen all evening, mooning about and smoking a lot?"

"Well, yes, sir," he answered slowly. "Hi did say that. The marster did happear to be a bit 'opped lawst night. But bless you, a guy gets that way sometimes. Hand the marster halways smokes ha goodish bit."

Jim nodded. "An' I guess that's right," he agreed. "He was

beefin' over wantin' his own brand of tobacco at the jail this mornin."

"Yes, sir." Kingsley smiled faintly. " 'E Smokes a very special brand 'e does—both 'e hand Mr. George, 'is brother, sir. Now hand then I scrags a pipeful myself. But the marster don't mind. 'E's a toff like I said."

"Forgetting that for a moment," I switched the subject, "and forgetting last night also, have you noticed any change in your master the last month?"

Kingsley eyed me almost as though for a personal hurt. "There you go again, sir," he said. "Hand hif the bobbies think him balmy. Hi don't like to say a word. But 'e 'as changed a bit from w'at he was. Hothers besides me must 'ave noticed hit, sir, from the way you talk. 'E 'asn't been as cheerful, hif you know w'at I mean—like, as hif 'e 'ad somethink hon 'is mind, hand a bit quick to get 'is wind up, a bit 'ard to please."

"Did you know that he had quarreled with Miss Mason?" I asked.

"Quarreled with 'er?" he repeated in surprise. "No, sir. 'E halways spoke of 'er hin the most affectionate fashion. Fair gorn on 'er 'e was. You're sure there 'ad been words between them?"

I nodded. "She told us so herself."

Kingsley frowned, and then he brightened. "But she's for 'im. She must be for 'im, hif she come to you to 'elp 'im. Het couldn't 'ave been serious," he said.

"Miss Mason understands, that is, she fears that for some time Mr. Lamb has not been quite himself."

"Gor bless me!" Kingsley seemed very much disturbed. That the man had been and was fond of his employer, the man who had saved his life, had taken him in and given him employment, when he was no more than a bit of human flotsam of war, one could no longer doubt. He worked for Lamb, but aside from any question of mere employment, one sensed that his service was sincerely a service of loyalty.

"There hisn't hany reason for hit. Hunless—my word, sir, do

you fawncy hit could 'ave come from the time a Fritz bashed him in the conk, that time 'e crashed his plane be'ind their lines?"

"As to that, I don't know," I said with a glanced at Jim. "Almost anything can happen from that sort of thing, I believe, according to medical men. Suppose you tell us exactly what happened last night as well as you can remember."

"Hi can remember hall right," he declared. "Right hafter twelve hit was. Hi was gettin' ready to turn hin. Hi 'ears a noise like my door bein' hopened, hand Hi turns around, hand hit was the marster, with a funny look hon 'is mush hand ha gun hin 'is 'and.

" 'Hello!' Hi says, not realizin' Wat was hup, hand thinkin' maybe 'e wanted to speak with me. But 'e doesn't say a word. 'E comes hat me scowlin' somethin' fierce, hand makin' ha funny noise hin 'is throat. Like a growl hit was. Hand 'e grabs me, hand bashes me one hon the crumpet with the butt of the gun. Fair staggered Hi was with the blow hand surprise.

"But Hi grabs 'is gun wrist, hand we fought hall hover the room. 'E's strong—a fine athlete han' swimmer as you may 'ave noticed—broad in the shoulders, with 'ips has lean has a 'ound's. But hi 'eld hon to 'im, callin' lim by name. Hi says. 'Mr. Himer, for heaven's sake w'at's the matter?' But 'e doesn't 'eed me, hand Hi thinks my time 'as come till a Mr. Blackmore hin the hapartment next door 'ears the racket, hand comes hand busts the glass hin the front door, hand let's 'imself hin.

"You may 'ave seen, sir, that there hare several little panes. 'E busts one, hand hunlocks the door hand runs hin, pulls Mr. Himer orf me, hand between us we tie 'im hup, hand call the police. They takes 'im away, hand I goes arfter a doctor, 'as my 'ead tied hup, hand comes back again.

"Then this mornin' Mr. George comes to see me, hand says ham Hi goin' to make trouble for Mr. Himer, hand Hi tells 'im my word no—I can't do nuthink like that, me howin' Mr. Himer my life, hand honly bein' worried habout 'is seemingly goin' orf 'is mind.

"So Mr. George says 'e's glad I feel like that hand for me to stick hit 'ere till 'e sees 'ow heverythink his comin' hout. Hi tells 'im Hi will, hand 'e goes orf, hand Hi laven't 'eard a bloomin' word from hany one till you come. Hi can't hunderstand hit, hi cawn't."

"As a matter of fact, Kingsley," I said, "Nobody quite understands it at this time. It's rather odd for him to suddenly change and attack you after you've been friends for years. But I believe that is one symptom of such things. You say Lamb paid no attention when you called him by name, and said nothing before he attacked you?"

"No, sir, 'e didn't," Kingsley returned. "Hit's my opinion that 'e didn't know me. The way hit himpressed me, 'e mought 'ave thought me hanother man. Hand hafter Mr. Blackmore hand me 'ad tied 'im hup hand was waitin' for the police, 'e simply sat starin' hand tryin' now hand then to pull 'imself loose. 'E wasn't 'imself, sir. Hi'll take my oath to that."

"You've got the gun?" Bryce questioned as the valet paused, and sat regarding us with a troubled frown.

"No, sir." He shook his head. "The police took hit with them w'en they took Mr. Himer. But hit was one Mr. Himer 'ad during the war. Ha sort of relic hit was."

I looked at Jim, and he nodded and rose. There was nothing to be learned here in the opinion of us both. Nothing that save what was indicated to support the belief of Dr. Simpson that Imer Lamb was mentally unsound. Seemingly he had made a murderous and unprovoked attack on a man whose life he had saved, a man he had befriended for years.

Outside of the assumption that there was some change in the man himself, the thing did not balance up. Of Kingsley's attitude toward Lamb there could be no doubt. One could see that in the inner, recesses of Kingsley's soul, Imer Lamb was pretty much his god.

"W'at are they goin' to do with 'im, sirs?" he questioned as he brought our hats. "Are they goin' to turn 'im hout?"

"Hardly, I'm afraid," I told him. "Not now at least. It's far more likely that they'll put him in the county hospital for observation, Kingsley, until they at least decide whether he will be safe to release or not."

"The 'orspital," he repeated. "Then Hi'll be packin' 'is bags. 'E'll need clean linen, 'e will, hand hevery think else. Most like Hi'll 'ear from Mr. George."

"Probably," I agreed. "That's not a bad thought, about packing his bags. He'll need fresh clothing, of course."

"Yes, sir. Thank you, sir," he accepted my approval of his suggestion. "Hi'll hattend to hit at once. Good arfternoon, sirs." He opened the door for us to pass.

We descended to the street. It was half past two o'clock.

And now Bryce suggested, "I suppose the next thing we do is see George. I don't know what good it can do. But orders is orders, as the soldier boys remark. Still, if Imer Lamb ain't crazy he's givin' a darned fine imitation of a man who is. Seems too bad.

"If that lad up there is telling the truth, and for one I don't doubt it, Lamb's been a real guy in the past. That checks up with what Miss Mason says, too—gentle an' strong was about the way she summed Imer up. Funny how a chap with about everything a man could want, from plenty of jack to a swell little dame ready to hop over the stick with him any time they was mutually ready, should have blown up. Funny thing, the human brain."

I nodded. His words brought back to my mind the impression Moira Mason had made upon me that morning of a sunbeam dimmed by a cloud, and called up the cloud of trouble that had lurked in the limpid depths of her blue eyes, of the set tension of repression that had ridden upon her flower-like mouth.

Moira Mason and Kingsley both were suffering. Both were troubled in their brains because of the wreck which had occurred in the brain of the man each in his or her own way loved. It was a strange thing, the brain—that laboratory in which were generated the impulses that drove us to sane or insane deeds.

"Yes, Jim," I said. "And apparently Lamb's has gone wrong.

As to what good we're doing I can't say. At least though we got Dual the hour of the man's arrest. With that to go on he can erect a preliminary, what he calls a horary figure of what took place, and govern his future actions from what he reads. We've known him to do that before, and I think that's what he intends doing in the present instance, and I suspect he is only doing it because Miss Mason asked for what information he could give."

"Tough," said Jim. "Tough on the girl, and tough on Lamb himself. If anybody I was fond of was to get batty in the belfry I'd rather they was dead, I guess."

"They'd be better dead," I declared. "Lamb's life can't hold much for him from now on, if he really is. Incarceration in some institution for the criminally insane is about what he has to expect."

"Yep!" my partner agreed. "An' if that ain't just about a livin' death, I don't know what is."

We walked to a corner and caught a trolley car bound for the business section; left it in the financial district, where banks, trust companies and brokerage firms crowded stone and brick and terra cotta shoulders, and looked for the Lamb address.

Presently we found it. "Lamb & Lamb" the firm name glinted back at us from heavy plate-glass windows, in letters of burnished gilt.

"Here we are." Bryce laid his hand to the door, and we passed from the glare of the street into a semi shadowed interior of a tile and marble foyer, to proffer our request for an interview. In doing so we took a leaf from our experience at Monk's Hall, and declared ourselves friends of Miss Mason.

"Mr. Lamb is engaged at present," the girl at the information desk said. "Shall I send in your names?"

"If you please," I decided. "We'll wait."

We turned away to where a leather-upholstered divan ringed the base of a massive pillar, and sat down. The offices of Lamb & Lamb were rather sumptuous, all marble, mahogany, and brass. At the end of the foyer in which we sat was a bank of private rooms. I fixed my eyes on that bearing the designation: "Mr. George Lamb."

Presently that door opened, and a woman emerged—a woman handsomely groomed, a beautiful woman, in a darkly sophisticated way.

"Good-by," she spoke over her shoulder in a well-modulated voice.

Then she was coming toward us with a graceful step, a faint smile on her carmined lips. She was wholly self-possessed, thoroughly poised, if one might judge by her bearing. She passed us closely, and I saw Jim's glance follow her slender retreating back. Then his voice was in my ears:

"Know who that was?"

I shook my head, turning my eyes from the woman just vanishing into the street.

"Nathalie Norton," he told me, mentioning a name I recognized as that of a girl who had won considerable popularity on the screen some seasons before, but of whom I had heard little of late. "You know George is interested in the Acme Film Distributing Corporation. Maybe Nathalie's makin' a play to get back in the pictures. Well, she wasn't so bad. I used to sort of like to see her stuff myself."

I nodded. Jim had a rather heterogeneous collection of information concerning all sorts of people in his head. Right now, however, I was more interested in watching the girl at the information desk.

As Bryce paused, she signed to us that we might seek Lamb in his room. I nodded again to indicate that I understood, and got up.

"Come along, Jim," I said.

He followed me back to the door of the room Nathalie Norton had just left. I rapped upon it.

"Come in," called a somewhat irascible voice.

I pushed the door open, and we went in.

George Lamb sat at a desk. He was as different from his

brother as day from night. Where Imer was darkly handsome, George was blond and heavy-set, with grayish blue eyes that swept Bryce and me in a fashion one instantly felt was antagonistic, even before he spoke:

"Well, gentlemen? Mr. Glace and Mr. Bryce, isn't it? Friends of Miss Mason, I think you said? Hasn't that girl sense enough not to send you down here at such a time?"

"If by 'at such a time' you refer to your foster brother's condition and his present incarceration, do you find it strange that the woman who has been engaged to him for some time should take an interest in the matter, Mr. Lamb?" I returned.

For a moment he stared, and then he half rose from his chair, and again subsided within it.

"Well," he said, "we won't argue about it. You're here now; so sit down, and be brief. Just what is it that you and Moira Mason want? Or, wait! Before you answer that, suppose you tell me who you two really are?"

CHAPTER V

SURLY GEORGE

IT WAS AN inauspicious opening to our interview. Two things were evident from the first. George Lamb was nervously on edge, and he appeared very apprehensive about the purpose of our visit. The first was not surprising, considering the fact that Imer was in jail with a strong probability of being adjudged mentally unbalanced.

But the second was not so ready to explain, in view of the fact that in so far as he knew we came to him from the woman his foster brother had expected to make his wife, a girl to whom I had been very strongly attracted as one of a splendid personality.

Because of that I sought to draw him out still further before I gave him any information affecting Jim's and my interest in Imer Lamb's affairs.

"Whether we are friends of Miss Mason or not, Mr. Lamb," I rejoined, "I feel that I may assume that you do not entertain a similar feeling for the lady yourself."

"I do not." He literally bit off the words. "Never have—never expect to."

"Then you did not approve of your brother's engagement, of course?" I remarked.

"Absolutely not!" he declared, still with unmistakable emphasis.

"May one ask why?" I questioned, further keeping my eyes on his face.

It darkened. The man scowled.

"It's none of your damned business, you know," he snarled. "Now, instead of sitting there asking questions, you answer a few or get out. Who are you?"

"Glace and Bryce," I told him. "I'm Glace. My companion is Mr. James Bryce, my partner. We are private investigators, Mr. Lamb. But—"

"Private investigators!" He nearly shouted. "Private investigators of what?"

"Of anything that needs investigating, Mr. Lamb," I resumed. "But, as I remarked before, if you will let me finish my explanation, I hope we can get together rather than pulling at cross-purposes."

"Get together? How do you mean, get together?" he demanded, staring at me across his desk. "D'ye mean that fool girl asked you to investigate my brother's—what happened at Monk's Hall last night?"

"Not exactly," I tried to continue my explanation. "As a matter of fact, our position in business has nothing at all to do with this. You misunderstand us, I'm afraid. Miss Mason came to see us this morning with Mrs. Robert Harding, who has known us for years. Naturally Mr. Imer Lamb's arrest had left her very much perturbed. I say naturally because it is natural, Mr. Lamb. You're a bit on edge yourself."

He breathed deeply. I saw his chest rise and fall. And then he visibly relaxed. He nodded.

"You're right there, Mr. Glace, I am," he said in more quiet fashion. "But if you're not here as investigators of something that I can't see needs either investigation or any more publicity than can be avoided, why in hell are you here?"

And right there I decided it was time to make things as clear as I could, to tell him the literal truth, no matter whether once I had done it the man would understand or not.

Dual had placed no embargo on my talking, had given me no instructions save to visit the jail and Monk's Hall and Lamb. Having made my way into the presence of the latter, I did not believe that he would possibly be anything more than surprised at my narrative, but in what I had to tell I judged might lie a means of catching his at least temporary interest.

"If you'd give me a chance to explain," I said, and smiled.

"I've been trying to get you to do it," he rejoined shortly. "Go on."

I complied. At last I had the chance. I recounted briefly Moira Mason's visit to us that morning, and her subsequent interview with Semi Dual, and his promise to tell her on the morrow what he thought. And at last Lamb heard me without interruption—though, as I proceeded, his expression altered, became that of one faintly amused, and at the end he laughed in a fashion little short of a sneer.

"And that girl does that—comes to you and gets you to take her to this star-gazing fortune teller of yours? You want me to believe that? Rot, Glace, bunk! It's too large a wad to swallow, though I'm not denying it's the sort of hokum that might appeal to her.

"She's a butterfly—just a butterfly. And the devil of it is that the last few years Imer's been butterflying himself. I've wanted him to settle down and apply himself to our business, but he's been satisfied to 'let George do it.' And that's no joke. To me at least it's been an unsatisfactory truth. Well, that's that.

"For the rest of it, how does your story justify your forcing your way in on me? Does your principal imagine you may collect enough dope from the visit to enable him to stall along with her?"

"He ain't stallin', brother," Bryce said gruffly, Lamb's decidedly offensive manner having apparently moved him to speech.

"No?" The broker stared. "You aren't trying to sell me the idea that you think he's genuine, are you? Listen. I cut my wisdom teeth early, and I've got all four of 'em yet."

"I ain't tryin' to sell you nuthin'," Jim told him, beginning to grow a bit red in the face. "I don't suppose any one could sell you so much as a thought that there may be things you never heard of in your life. That aside, I've heard of cases where a man's teeth affected not only his hearing, but his sight.

"Personally, Glace and I have known Semi Dual for years, an' watched his work. I didn't believe it any more than you do at first, but I'm sold now, and I'm a fairly stubborn guy myself.

"I used to be a bull before I went in with Glace. But since then Dual's helped us clear up more than one muddle, an' he's even helped the police. If you don't want to take my word, ask Johnson of the Central Office. He's come to us to ask for that sort of help just like that girl did this morning. An' he got what he come for too. Now try an' laugh that off."

"Well, by Heaven!" Once more Lamb's expression altered, showed genuine surprise, and something else, a vague puzzlement perhaps. He frowned. In some degree at last he seemed impressed. Jim's rumbling defiance of his opinion couched in language he could not fail to understand seemed to have caught his attention, held it, and even raised a question he sought to answer and failed. He rasped out his half profane exclamation and paused, and then went on again. "So that's who you are. You used to be Inspector Bryce. I remember you now. You weren't a fool either, from all accounts, in those days. You—"

Jim interrupted. "Don't let the idea that I'm one now run away with you, George. This thing boils down to this. Things happen, an' you an' me don't always know why. But this stuff Dual believes in and puts into practice shows why it did, I don't mean maybe."

"Apparently not," Lamb said. He forced a smile, but I noted that his frown still lingered in his eyes. "However, I'm afraid that we've been wasting time in a discussion that is leading nowhere. Just what is it you want to know about my brother? I still can't see that it affects either you or your friend to any justifiable extent, but—put it into words."

"Do you," I said, "know of anything bearing directly on the incidents of last night, any reason why your brother, Imer, should have chosen Kingsley his valet, any reason why he should have tried to assault any one?"

"Naturally, I don't," he declared without hesitation. "If I'd even dreamed that Imer was on the verge of running amuck, I'd have taken steps to keep him under restraint."

"You would have?" I questioned.

"Certainly," he returned with a sigh that smacked of exasperation. "I hope, Mr. Glace, you don't think I'm one to let a man with a homicidal mania run at large."

"You know about Dr. Simpson's belief that it is homicidal mania, then?" I suggested.

"Know about it?" he repeated. "Of course, I know about it. As soon as I knew about what happened last night I tried to get my brother out on bail; saw Kingsley, got his assurance that he wouldn't appear against him, and then bumped into Simpson's version of the matter; and failed, of course."

Suddenly he shrugged his shoulders and laughed again without any sound of humor. "Oh, there's reason enough why I'm not quite myself this afternoon. Simpson insists on holding him for observation. Nice thought, my brother—kid I grew up with—stuck into some public institution with a lot of common bums and thugs."

"I can understand that," I assented. "But under the conditions there is little you can do about it, I suppose."

"I don't know, Glace." He pursed his full lips in an expression of consideration. "I don't know yet, for sure—that is. There, may be a way out. I've a little influence. I may be able to get Imer turned over to me—get the privilege of keeping him in a private institution if Simpson decides he's right inside the next few days. Right now that's about the best I can hope for, so far as I can see."

"If your influence is strong enough to turn the trick?" Bryce said as Lamb once more paused.

Lamb nodded. "Sure. But I think it is."

"Then it would be your best bet, if a commission decides that Simpson's right," Jim agreed. "Would you get yourself appointed his guardian, or what?"

"Guardian?" Lamb appeared to consider the suggestion.

"Why, I hadn't thought of that. It could be done, I suppose. But I can't see any need. Technically Imer and I are partners, even if he does hardly ever come in down here. What I mean, though, as applying to your question, is that Imer's money is in the business jointly with my own.

"I've looked after the business end of his share of the estate for years. So I don't see where the necessity of taking out guardianship papers would come in. I can't see why things should not continue as they are as long as his share of the income is sufficient to supply his needs."

"Not as long as you're practically in charge of his affairs already," said Bryce.

"Not only practically, but actually, Mr. Bryce." For the third time Lamb laughed. "Ever since he came out of the army Imer has done little but play about. That's the real reason I was opposed to his marrying Miss Mason. I've nothing against the girl herself; but I don't consider her the type of woman for his wife.

"I would have liked to see him marry some girl who would have stimulated his ambition. Oh, he has ambition if it could be waked up. He made a good record in the war. But since then he's gone head over heels into sports, tennis, golf, motor racing, aviation here of late. He did a bit of that while he was in the service, as you may have heard.

"But a woman can keep a man on the ground as well as lift him to the skies. And it's the ground sort of woman Imer ought to have—the sort of woman who would stimulate him to get in and dig, instead of being content to 'let George do it,' as I said before, and live off the income of the money his father made."

"Maybe he thinks that's only a fair break after all," Bryce observed. "Didn't old Lamb leave you half his estate?"

"He did," Lamb replied. "And I'm not kicking, Mr. Bryce. What I've really been trying to put into words is that I've wanted Imer to do something more than dawdle his time away, for his own good. Life isn't all play, Mr. Bryce. I've felt he ought to do something worth while."

"Still," Jim persisted, "practically, I can't see that it really matters so long as you do enough for both."

Lamb turned his glance toward him briefly.

"Well, I don't know that it does," he said.

The telephone beside him on the desk emitted a purr. He turned toward it, answered, listened, and spoke. "Tell 'em to wait. I'll be through in a few minutes."

Replacing the receiver, he turned again to Bryce. "On the whole, I'm not sure but it's fortunate the way things have turned out. If Imer had done what I wanted, he'd have left me up in the air. There would have been things, details of business, with which I wouldn't have been in touch. This way—well—I've all the threads in my fingers. And I'm up to my neck in one or two big deals."

"You're in the Acme Film, aren't you?" Jim said.

There were times when he had an impudent nerve. Now, as it seemed to me, he might as well have asked Lamb the reason for Nathalie Norton's presence in his office when we arrived. My mind harked back to the woman, even as I awaited Lamb's reply.

"Acme Film?" I thought he narrowed his lids, that just for an instant they hooded his eyes; and then for the fourth time he laughed. "Nathalie Norton make you think of that, Mr. Bryce?"

Jim nodded. A half grin twitched at his mouth.

"Thought she might be comin' back into pictures," he confessed. "The Acme used to distribute her stuff, didn't it?"

"It did." Lamb leaned back in the chair in which he sat. For a moment he said nothing more, and then he resumed in what seemed a complacent voice: "But Nathalie isn't thinking of coming back at present. She just dropped in to see me. She's an intimate friend of mine."

For a moment Bryce sat puffing out his stubby toothbrush mustache, and then he struck back verbally at Lamb's air of aplomb:

"Why have you been urgin' marriage on your brother?"

"I haven't been urging marriage on him," Lamb snapped. "I've merely told you the sort of woman I felt he ought to marry if he wanted a wife."

I thought of what Jim had said that morning about a good woman being the finest product of her race, and the other sort being the worst influence in the world; but I said no word. Once more the picture of Nathalie Norton swam before my mental eyes. And then again I heard Bryce:

"I guess we'll be on our way, an' let you go on with your work." He stood up, and I rose to my feet too.

"That," said Lamb, as he reached for the telephone standard, "is a mutually happy thought. Good afternoon, Mr. Glace and Mr. Bryce."

"Toodle-oo," said Jim and turned to the door.

I followed him out.

Outside he exploded into the righteous indignation of a real man. "The dirty scut! For two cents I'd go back and spread my fist over his map. I was a bull for years, an' I seen enough then; but George makes me sick. Take a long breath an' get some clean air into your lungs. Breathe deep, son, breathe deep. On the level, if I had my choice of bein' one of them two I'd choose to be Imer on his past record, even if they are going to put him in the foolish house."

I nodded. I felt a good deal the same myself. George Lamb had impressed me unpleasantly from the first, and toward the last he had actually affected me with a sense akin to nausea.

"Speaking of Imer, it occurs to me that being as prominent an amateur sportsman as he has been, there should be more than a little interest shown in his case. Let's buy a paper, and see what they say about it."

Jim hailed a newsboy with a late afternoon edition, and bought one of the still damp sheets.

Then standing there together on a corner we ran through it,

seeking for any public mention of the man in whom we had come to feel an interest, and after a time we found it:

IMER LAMB VICTIM OF HOMICIDAL
MANIA, CITY PHYSICIAN SIMPSON SAYS

CHAPTER VI

SEMI DUAL LISTENS

THE STORY ITSELF was no more than a rehash of the arrest of Lamb the night before, plus a very complete play-up of the man's record in the world of amateur sport. There followed the statement of the city alienist, and the information that Lamb had that afternoon been transferred to the County Hospital observation ward. We read it, and Bryce folded up the paper, thrusting it into a pocket of his coat.

"And except for one thing that would settle the matter," he declared. "If Moira Mason hadn't come to us this morning, an' Dual hadn't taken an interest in this affair, why, Imer would be as good as tended to, I guess."

I nodded. Save for the intervention of the woman—the clouded sunbeam girl, as I persisted in thinking of her—Imer Lamb's life in so far as his fellow man was concerned would be as good as closed, since even though his body went on living, the real man, now that reason had tottered on her throne in his fellow man's opinion, the Imer Lamb who had been had died.

"Let's go tell him about Kingsley and George," said Bryce.

"All right," I agreed.

We went back, entered the foyer of the Urania, and caught an express car to the top. Side by side we mounted the bronze and marble stairs. Beside the fountain in the shadow of the tower cast by the westering sun was seated a figure in purple and white; Semi Dual sat there in seeming meditation, which he broke as the annunciator chimes rang out.

"My friends," he said, lifting his deep gray eyes as we approached and smiling slightly. "My friends, who have been as feet for me, while the soul of me has worked, so that ye have traveled while I have sat and thought. Tell me that which I perceive now has been not wholly to your liking."

Bryce fumbled in a pocket, produced a cigar, and lowered himself to the seat beside the fountain basin in which tiny goldfish flitted to and fro like vagrant flecks of the sunlight that was gilding the rest of the roof.

I followed suit.

And then we told the man who had sent us forth what we had done, omitting no detail we could recall, however slight. He listened, sunk again, as it appeared from his posture and his utter quiet, into his mood of meditation between us on the carved stone bench.

On and on our voices droned, reciting scraps of conversation, describing incidents.

"They transferred Lamb to the County Hospital this afternoon," I remarked.

"Into invisible bondage," Dual made comment, half as it seemed to us and half to himself.

"Eh? Invisible?" Bryce repeated.

"The bonds of the soul are invisible, unseen. And he whose soul, whose self, is enchained in such fashion is lost indeed—unless some soul agency intervenes."

"Some soul agency?" I revoiced the syllables that gave me that impression of widening circles spreading out—spreading out just beyond the reach of my pursuing mind.

"The law of the universe, rather than any law of man, my friend."

Love, a soul agency, intervention! The picture of Moira Mason swam before my mental vision again; Imer Lamb would seem to have won her love at least. Had her coming, through us, to the man who sat now beside me been the beginning of the intervention he meant?

If so, then since we had left him this morning he must have learned something by his own peculiar methods toward the formulating of that opinion he had promised the golden-haired, blue-eyed little fiancée of Imer Lamb.

"Semi," I said, "you've learned something?"

"Not much," he said. "Of course, I have erected a horary figure of the assault Lamb made on his valet, after you telephoned me the hour of the call for his arrest. From that I might learn something, since each incident in life is but the result of causes constantly at work; Imer Lamb's attack upon the man whom he has befriended, whose life he saved, was the effect of causes leading inevitably to it, no matter how causeless it appears.

"Some shadowing of those causes I have discovered, crossed threads of meaning which, as I sat here before you came, I was seeking to coördinate."

"But this here now 'horary' figure, as you call it, would at least have shown whether Lamb was off his head when he made his attack on Kingsley," Bryce suggested. "Shown his condition at that time, I mean."

"Oh, yes," Semi Dual agreed. "At the time he attacked the man Imer Lamb was insane, in the sense in which modern man uses the term. He was insane; had been verging on insanity for some time. To that extent Dr. Simpson is right in the practice of his craft. More than that I would not care to say until I have gone more fully into my consideration of his case."

"You mean you think he may recover, break these here invisible bonds you were speakin' of?" Bryce said.

"I do not know," Dual answered slowly. "That must depend largely upon the causes which have led up to the present instance, I think."

"But—" Jim began, and sat frowning.

"You are thinking of the woman who came to me this morning," Semi Dual said as he paused. "To her I made a promise, and I shall redeem it in whatsoever manner I may. To that end, tonight I shall work, aided by what you have told me, and by what I shall read in yet other figures bearing on the question which troubles her soul, which I shall synthesize before the appointed hour. Bring her to me at that time."

The strange man on the bench in his white and purple robes, who read in the very sweep of the stars the mandates of the law of cause and effect in which he believed, had confirmed the opinion of the physician already broadcasted through the city in printer's ink; Imer Lamb was insane. His body had become no more than a house of bondage, his brain no more than a dwelling place, through the familiar corridors of which his soul struggled—no longer a free thing, but a thing dragging an invisible ball and chain, enslaved to Heaven knew what forces.

As I gained my feet and Bryce rose also, Dual spoke again a final parting assurance.

"Yet justice shall be done, my friends, and the law shall take its course."

We left him sitting there in his white and purple robes, and went down the path and the stairway, Bryce stalking beside me in silence, his cigar fast between his teeth.

And all at once Bryce spoke: "Justice can't afford to give much heed to Mercy. It wouldn't be justice if she did. An' the first thing we knew, instead of wearin' a bandage over her eyes, she'd be shedding glycerin tears."

It was like Bryce to say a thing like that. There was always about him a hard-headed facetiousness. None knew better than I that he had been stirred in no small measure by the half hour we had spent with the man we had just left, by the words that man had spoken, or that it was that very fact which dictated the turn of the comment he had just voiced. I thought a lot of Bryce, knew him as one knows a man with whom he has worked shoulder to shoulder for years.

I smiled at him now as we stood waiting for an elevator that came humming up the shaft. Once more we were back in the modern, everyday world.

"Just the same," exploded Jim, "I'd rather it was Dual than me had to tell that girl that Imer's off his nut."

That was like Jim, too. He had a big, and at times almost romantic heart under his bluff exterior.

Back in the office he referred to the matter again. "Imer's bughouse," he says, and then says that justice will be done an' the law will take its course. Now, what in times does he mean? If Imer's crazy, where is there any reason for pulling justice in, and what's the law got to do with the thing?

"Just between you and me I wouldn't trust that foster brother of his any farther than I could sling a flivver by the crank."

"You're right, Jim," I said.

Jim nodded. "Go on, call up Miss Mason, an' tell her to come here in the morning."

"Listen," I said, as I put out my hand for the telephone. "Is there any trouble with Acme Film?"

"Huh!" Bryce nearly dropped his cigar from between his lips, then caught it and clamped it back between his teeth again. "I dunno, but it might bear looking into. George handles the whole business—says he has all the threads in his fingers. He said that when I asked him if he'd try to get himself appointed Imer's guardian. An' he's the sort of man will bear watchin', or I ought to be back in harness pounding pavements again."

"I think so," I assented. To me it seemed that one of those widening ripples of meaning had at last been in a measure overtaken by my pursuing brain. Yet even so, its meaning was not plain. As yet it defied and baffled, was too vague for me to read. But it was there; I sensed it even though I could not define it. It was there.

"Which—that I'm right or ought to be back in harness?" Bryce grinned.

"Suit yourself," I told him, and took up the telephone standard to call Marya Harding and ask her to bring Moira Mason to us the next morning without fail.

"Mr. Glace, has Mr. Dual learned something?" she cried the moment I had proffered Semi's request.

"I don't know," I told her. "Not definitely, but I think so, Mrs. Harding."

"What does he say?" she demanded. "Tell me what he says, at least."

"He says justice shall be done, and the law shall take its course," I repeated Semi's assurance.

"Justice and law," she repeated. "What does he mean by it, Mr. Glace?"

I could almost feel her brain straining, even as mine was straining toward an understanding of the involved meaning. But I couldn't tell her.

"I don't know, Mrs. Harding, but he doesn't squander words," I said.

CHAPTER VII

MORIA AND THE WIZARD

I GOT TO the office early the next morning. But even so, Jim was before me, a look of expectancy on his face, and his inevitable cigar clamped fast between his teeth.

"I saw Johnson and told him what Semi said, an' it sent him up in the air without a parachute to get down on," he announced the moment we were together.

"Well, Johnson's the law," I said.

"Huh?" Jim stared. Then he nodded. "Well, I see what you mean; in a way he is. Anyway, there's going to be a commission appointed to examine Imer today. With Simpson standin' pat, that's merely a formality, Johnson seems to think. That's why he can't seem to see into that law and justice thing of Dual's. I left him chewin' on it."

"Naturally," I said, "since you couldn't help him yourself."

Bryce grinned. And then he sobered. "Nice day," he remarked, walking to a window, and staring out at a cloudless sky. "Too nice a day to be committed to that 'invisible bondage,' as Semi calls it."

He turned back to me again. "I'm interested in what lies back and behind what Semi's going to say to that girl this morning. When she comes I'm going up there with you, if you don't mind."

I nodded. "Sure, Jim," I said. "Come along if you like."

An hour passed before Moira Mason came.

Then Marya Harding brought her as on the day before.

"Marya told me what your strange friend said last evening," she said, as she gave me her hand. "I mean about justice and law. And I puzzled over it all night long. You still have no idea what he meant?"

"No clear idea, Miss Mason," I returned. "But I'm sure he meant something that time will make plain."

"You know that Imer is to go before a commission this morning?" she said with a little catch in her breath, and a quivering mouth.

"Yes'm," Bryce assured her before I could answer. "But that's just routine. Wouldn't you like to go up now an' see what Dual says?"

"Oh, yes, yes. Let's go," she assented. "I want to hear it, to know the best—or the worst—at once."

Jim and I took the two ladies up to the sun-bathed garden. Moira Mason fairly ran up the stairs from the twentieth floor to the roof.

As before, Dual sat beside the fountain. Only now he had provided shade for his guests against the sun's increasing heat, an awning of heavy striped silk, supported on slender poles.

Seen so in his robes of white and purple, with his splendid head and well-trimmed beard, he might have been some desert chieftain. And even like one, as we reached him, he put out both hands to Moira Mason, and she laid her hands in them, and looked up into his bending face.

"My child," he said. "My child, through the night I have beheld thee ever shining through my work, and now I see thy face, thou lamp of life through whom perchance light may even yet illumine a darkened house."

I caught at his words, and glanced at Marya Harding and at Bryce. Marya's lips were parted, and Jim's eye met mine in a quickening flash. Yesterday the strong man holding the hands of the girl we had brought to him, had likened the brain of a man to a house; now he was likening her to a lamp through which light might shine in it again.

She seemed to sense his meaning dimly. Her lips parted. She breathed deeply. Under the soft summer fabric that veiled it, I saw the quick rise and fall of her soft breast.

"You mean that—" she began. "That the brain of man may be a house of invisible bondage, unless some other soul shall strike off its chains?"

We found seats, Marya Harding and Moira, on the carved stone bench, Bryce and I on the rim of the fountain where the goldfish played. Dual stood between us. We sat like students at the feet of a master.

"Three of you who come to me this morning," spoke the sage, "know of my faith in the soundless voice of the stars. Therefore I have questioned them as to the why and wherefore of the thing which has come upon Imer Lamb. I have constructed astral charts dealing with the nativity of Imer Lamb himself, and of you, Miss Mason. And I have set up a figure dealing with the events of night before last. And now, as I pledged myself to do, I shall give you in part at least the message of the stars.

"The Moon and Mercury in the nativity of Imer Lamb are in favorable aspect to the sign of the ascendant. This means little to you, but to me it says that Imer Lamb, though insane—though about to be adjudged insane—"

"Adjudged insane!" The words fell as a tense whisper from Moira Mason's lips.

Dual extended his hand palm upward, toward her. "Peace," he said in his mellow tones. "Peace, my child. Are not the fingers of the soul Faith and Hope? Man judges his fellow man in his wisdom. Yet the wisdom of man too often is of the earth, earthy. Tune thy ear to the wisdom of other spheres."

"But—but don't you see? If they adjudge him insane they will—"

"They will lead him to a House of Invisible Bondage," said Semi Dual.

"Marya!" Moira Mason cried out, and turned to the woman

beside her, and hid her face against her, clinging to her, while a tremor of horror shook her.

I GLANCED at Bryce. A House of Invisible Bondage! I saw understanding in his eyes. Dual had voiced the finding of the commission that would examine Imer Lamb; he would be committed to the hospital for the insane.

Little Moira Mason's voice came again with a rasping sob.

Then Semi's voice: "Peace, Moira. I but said thy loved one should be adjudged insane, yet had ye not cried out I should have said that the condition is not one depending upon any definite change in the structure of his mind, upon no weakness of his brain."

"You mean he is not really insane!" Moira lifted herself from her posture against Marya Harding's body, and faced him with widening eyes.

"Nay." He shook his head slowly. "Trouble not yourself with my fuller meaning. Here let faith come in. For in the chart of his life we find Saturn afflicting his Mercury and Moon. This would incline to insanity, even though normally dormant, because of the favorable aspect of the last two elements named.

"Yet were something to fan it into life, this influence would excite insanity at night, and in the figure I have erected I find also Neptune in an evil configuration with the Lord of the Sixth House, also afflicting the ascendant and the conjoined Mercury and Moon. This could but aggravate Saturn's indication; and in these signs, in a measure at least, we find all that has happened, explained.

"Also Uranus is elevated above and to a minor degree afflicts both the Moon and Mercury, showing a tendency to some derangement of the mind.

"Mars is conjoined to Neptune. Consequently, by his aspect, Mars afflicts the same points as Neptune again. And here, at least, we have a material confirmation of the astral signs. Yesterday I asked you if Mr. Lamb drank. You replied that he smoked a great deal—and Neptune rules drugs which affect the nerves; and Mars rues tobacco, my child.

"Neptune inclines toward nerve affections of a certain type. Mars urges to murder, assault, and war. Mr. Lamb's assault on his man Kingsley resulted from a mental unbalance, and was of a murderous nature. Kingsley himself said that his employer fought night before last even as he himself had seen him fight when he was a member of the American Expeditionary Force."

Moira Mason nodded. "That was when he saved Joe Kingsley's life. He was brave. But if everything affects him—I thought you said—isn't there any hope at all?"

"Hope. Aye, Hope," said Semi Dual. And suddenly he smiled. "Let Hope support you; for have I not said that I have studied not only the figures of his nativity, but of yours? And in his, Venus, Jupiter, and the Sun throw their beneficent rays toward his Mercury and Moon, wherein once more is a plain meaning, that in the hour of his greatest need aid shall be given to him in as much as one of these modifying planets is ruler of the eleventh house.

"This is the House of Friends, out of which aid might best come in such a case. Jupiter is the orb of justice—and justice, thou troubled one, is a thing not easily swayed. And the Sun— happy he on whom it shines, from a favorable aspect."

"But Venus; you haven't assigned her a definite place." How closely the girl on the stone bench had followed his words were shown by her mention of his omission.

And once more Dual smiled. "Venus," he said. "Ah, yes, here enters Love. Venus, my child, in his life is thyself. For compar-

ing your astral charts, thy Jupiter once more offsets the evil of
his Saturn, while his Sun is on your ascendant, and shall thereby
give him of thy strength.

"Have I not called ye a Lamp? Have I not hinted that you
should light his life? Have I not counseled to Faith and Hope,
thou child of True Light? Strong though the forces be against
him; yet Love is the strongest force in life, since Life itself is but
the child of Love. Faith then, and Hope, and Love; herein is the
triad completed. Herein the three points of the triangle meet."

"Marya!" Once more Moira Mason cried out. "Marya! Do
you hear what he says? I am his Lamp of Life, his Hope! Oh,
heaven help us both!" Her arms lifted, she covered her face with
her fingers, and her shoulders shook.

"Aye," said Semi Dual. "See thy faith does not falter so that
his friendly signs work."

"His friendly signs?" She dropped her hands and looked him
in the face.

"Aye." For the third time Semi smiled upon her. "Thou Venus
and I Jupiter, with my satellites Glace and Bryce. Have I not said
that thy Jupiter overcame the evil of his Saturn, and was I not
brought into the matter through thy intervention in coming to
me in his behalf?

"And perhaps the Sun, perhaps the Law, the law which so
often lets in light upon the happenings in dark places should its
power be invoked will work."

Work. The word caught me up, with its implication of action
to be taken in the future, steps to be made. To me it seemed
that as never before Dual had taken a definite stand, assigned
himself a definite place.

I glanced at my partner. He sat leaning a trifle forward, the
stump of a dead cigar he had forgotten and let die out, clamped
in a corner of his mouth. His hand, next to me on the rim of the
fountain basin, was clamped upon it until the knuckles showed
white.

"I was talking to his brother," said Moira, "on the telephone, last night. He said he hoped that they might let him take charge of Imer and put him in some private institution, instead of sending him to an asylum run by the State."

"I think it quite probable that he will succeed in that endeavor," Semi declared.

"But he will come out again, be released, recover his reason?"

"Again in my estimation. It is to that end we shall work, thou, and I, and my friends, Glace and Bryce. And perchance, should the situation require it, should the need arise, justifying the action, perhaps others whom we shall call to our aid."

For the first time since Semi had begun his exposition of the astral position of the matter, Moira Mason turned her eyes to where Jim and I sat.

"You gentlemen will help him?" she said.

"Small need of your askin' that," Bryce answered that appeal on the instant. "All he's got to do is give his orders an' we'll carry 'em out, Miss Mason."

"And you, sir," she turned again to Semi, "I have money. Do what you can—everything. Spare no expense. As long as it lasts—"

"Nay," he interrupted. "I am blessed with means in plenty. But for my friends, who shall aid me, for their time and what expense shall be incurred, I accept thy aid. For in this matter it is written that Venus shall prove a friend of great assistance. So then I shall call upon you at the proper time. Meanwhile, possess thyself in faith. That which is to be will be; yet through thy intervention the course of what shall be has been changed. Encourage thy heart with this thought; and be not dismayed."

Moira Mason rose, and looked full into his face with its hint of unassailable strength. "In that faith you have given me, and the hope it inspires I shall wait for whatever happens," she said. "Mr. Bryce, will you lead me back to the everyday world?"

As he lifted himself from his seat, she smiled a smile of hope.

CHAPTER VIII

GETTING TOGETHER

"**KINGSLEY GAVE US** the lowdown that far anyway," Jim said as we watched Marya Harding and Moira Mason drive away, after escorting them down to their car. "The little girl's a bit of all right."

We went back to our office, and he began to rave. I think I might best describe it as that. He was as full of unshed words as the skin of an overstuffed sausage is of meat.

"Jupiter, Venus, and the Sun, Uranus, Neptune and Mars," he broke out the minute we were inside my private room and had closed the door. "The Moon an' Mercury are afflicted by the latter, an' I'm sick myself. My great grandmother's cat! What a constellation of stars. Faith, Hope, an' Love.

"If Semi's even half right about this thing, it looks like a free-for-all with no holds barred. Imer Lamb is crazy except for the fact that there's nothing the matter with his head—despite which he's billed through to a House of Invisible Bondage, an' it's our job to pry him out." He produced a cigar, bit off the end, and fumbled in a pocket without success. "Got a match?"

I gave him one. "All you have said is true," I remarked. "Your exposition of the matter is quite complete, and it's lucid as mud."

"Yes, ain't it?" Jim grinned as he lighted his cigar. "But the point is that it proves I was dead right."

"How come?" I suggested.

"Why about there bein' a lot more back an' behind this matter of Bo-Peep's Lamb than you can see on the face. The only trouble is we don't know what it is."

"Yes," I agreed, "that's the trouble. But then, both as a cop and later as a private detective, you may have found that frequently the case."

He nodded, grinning again. "Oh, yes," he admitted. "You're a funny fellow, Gordon. You're as humorous as a crutch. An' there's somethin' else funny. That's how Semi works. Ordinarily, if a man's crazy, he's crazy. It takes a man like Semi Dual to calmly announce that he's that way because a few antagonistic stars have put his Moon an' his Mercury on the blink. Well, that's that. Mercury rules the mind, I understand, an' th' Moon is the pet sign of our friends the lunatics.

"Only that ain't the point. What I mean is that if it wasn't for Semi, Imer would simply be slipped into some institution, an' the incident would be marked closed, as apparently it's not. An' Bo-Peep would be a widow without havin' been a wife, instead of drivin' off with the understandin' that as Venus she's got a chance to help get Imer sprung from the foolish house. Do you see what I'm drivin' at?"

"Perfectly, old boy," I told him.

"Semi says that justice is going to be done, which means that he sees even now a little bit deeper than he said, that he has at least some conception of what it's all about. And he told her just now that we were going to help him clear this matter; so that being the case it looks to me as though our part was simply to hold ourselves ready to carry out his orders—and meanwhile wait.

"In the main," he assented as I paused. "But not quite. I'm goin' to find out what I can about the Acme Film Company. I got a friend that's pretty well on the inside in pictures, an' I'm goin' to call on him an' have a talk."

"Still figuring on George?" I said as he stood up.

"I don't like him." He frowned the least bit. "I don't cotton to him m'son. Lookin' at it that way you might say I was prejudiced; but he owes what he has to Imer's old man, ever since he was a kid, an' I've noticed that his sort of a cur don't hesitate to bite the hand that feeds it.

"Gratitude is somethin' that dies darned quick when it happens to run against a man's self-conceit—an' George is conceited. He thinks he's the only skipper on the cheese. What I don't know is where he shows up in Semi's charts. But he must show somewhere. He's close to Imer. Dual said Saturn, Neptune, Uranus, Mars, was unfriendly to Lamb. I'm no astrologer, my boy, but I'd like to know which of them unfriendly four is George."

"You think he is one of them?" I questioned. As yet I had found no time in which to indulge in speculation as to Semi's deeper meaning, and my understanding of the subject was vague. Just the same Jim's suggestion gave me pause.

Roughly speaking I knew the characteristics assigned to the major planets, and I knew that the nature of Uranus was held to be explosive in type. Also I knew that both Uranus and Neptune revolved on their axes in a reverse direction from the earth. I had heard Dual state that Uranian and Neptunian natures were apt to defy earth-established conventions. A picture of Nathalie Norton and of George Lamb, as we had talked with him the day before, grew swiftly in my mind. I looked Jim in the eyes.

"I'll lay you a bet he's Uranus," he declared, confirming my silent surmise.

Jim left me to my speculations, starting on his self-determined investigation of Acme Film.

It was twelve o'clock. I put on my hat, and went out for lunch.

Bryce was in the office when I got back, and as usual he was smoking. But I could see no satisfaction in his face.

"Well," I said, "did you find out much about Acme?"

"I did. I reckon I found out all about it." He nodded. "I found out that George, and Imer, and a coupla movie picture magnates are Acme, an' its stock is quoted above par with none for sale, an' that they're distributing for what you might call the cream of the movie stars.

"An' speaking of stars, I found out enough to convince me that when it comes to readin' astrological indications, I'm apparently not the man for the job. Accordin' to my information, Gibraltar's a crumblin' ruin alongside Acme Film."

He seemed actually crestfallen about it, and I smiled. "Apparently then, Acme Film is a going concern," I suggested.

"That's it. It's goin' good." Jim scowled. "I let on to this party I went to see that I was thinkin' of pickin' up a few shares, an' he admitted it was a good thing to think if it could be done, the only trouble with the notion being that he didn't believe it could, in view of the fact that the Lambs an' these picture foundrymen had it all nailed down. He called it the same thing you do, a goin' concern. Seemed to think the best thing a guy could ask was a chance to go along."

"Then," I began, and paused as a heavy voice rumbled in the outer office; the door was pulled unceremoniously open, and Inspector Johnson stepped in.

"Hello," he said, as he made for a chair and lowered himself upon it. "Busy?"

"Not excessively," I confessed. "Jim, here, had an idea he thought a lot of till the thing blew up. But otherwise—"

"Most of his ideas are that way," Johnson interrupted.

"Huh?" Bryce grunted.

"Otherwise," Johnson gave him a grin. "Still, where ignorance is bliss—"

"Oh, Dora, keep your slams," Jim cut him short. "As a wisecracker you're the sort would think a firecracker something to eat. So, before you try to lay any pavements out of that bit of concrete you carry around on your shoulders, suppose you put us hep to what sort of information you expected to get by comin' up here."

"As a matter of fact, I come up with the notion of makin' a friendly visit," Johnson declared.

"You did?" Bryce eyed him. "Well, you're makin' a darned poor start. However, I've known you long enough to be willin' to take your word for it, no matter how you act. Just what was your notion of bein' friendly?"

"Why, this Imer Lamb," Johnson said. "Yesterday an' this mornin' you seemed to be takin' an interest in his case. He had his hearin' this mornin', an' they paroled him in the care of his brother. Thought you might like to hear th' result."

"Paroled him, did they?" Jim received the information.

I met his eyes; their lids were narrowed.

Johnson nodded. "Yep. His brother showed up at the hearing, an' offered to take care of him at his own expense. Put up a bond an' agreed to see that Imer had medical treatment an' all the rest of it. Naturally the commission didn't care, as long as the case was taken care of, an' of course it's that much less expense to the State. So they let Lamb take him."

"Where?" Bryce questioned.

"Out here. To Doc Drake's, I understand," Johnson returned. "At least that's what I understood he meant to do at the hearing. You know Drake's got a place out here in the Hillcrest addition—big house he took three or four years ago an' fixed up for his sort of work. Lamb agreed to take Imer out there an' turn him over to Drake. Didn't know whether you'd heard it yet or not."

"Nope." Jim shook his head. "We hadn't. But George said he had that sort of a move in his mind yesterday afternoon, like I told you this mornin'. Well, he seems to have put it across."

"Put it across?" Johnson repeated.

"Sure. Got Imer turned over to him instead of to the State," Bryce explained.

"Oh," Johnson said. "Well, I guess that's natural enough. The Lambs have bundles of money. There's no reason why George shouldn't fix it that way, is there?"

"None that I know of," said Bryce.

"Anyway," Johnson went on, "that does for Imer. Everything's all shipshape, open and aboveboard. What I can't see is how that justice and law stuff you were pullin' as comin' from your friend Dual this mornin' matches up."

So that was it. I looked at him and laughed. "Believe in reciprocity, don't you, Johnson?" I took a part in the conversation. "You come up here with the dope on Imer's being paroled to George an' literally railroaded into a private insane asylum; and I suppose Jim told you that Moira Mason had a date to meet Semi this morning when you two had your chat."

"Oh, well," he said, "I ain't denyin' that in view of how things turned out at the hearin' I've been wonderin' just how he'd look at it. I've worked a few times with him, as you know, an' though I've never been able to make him or his stuff I'm ready enough to admit that it ain't like him to be left holdin' th' sack. I asked Simpson after the hearing if these homicidal mania cases ever recovered, an' he let on it was mighty seldom."

Bryce cut in: "An' you was sort of hopin' that maybe for once you'd got Semi in a trap?"

"Oh, no." Johnson frowned. Though he had worked with Dual, had appealed to him through us for aid, Semi's work and his methods had always left him baffled, puzzled as he had said. One could hardly escape the feeling that he would not have been overwhelmed with sorrow had Dual actually made a slip. "It ain't that, Jim," he continued. "Not exactly. But what happened this mornin' seems sort of final."

"Yes, don't it?" Bryce mumbled about his cigar. "Not withstandin' which, I've an idea that if you was to ask him you'd find Dual standin' pat. He told Moira Mason they was goin' to lead Imer to a House of Invisible Bondage," said Jim. "An' I reckon that about describes this place of Drake's."

"Just about," Johnson assented. "Big house on a hill, with a lot of trees around it, an' a lot of its windows barred. Aside from that, what else did he tell her?"

"Oh, he told her plenty," Jim declared. His disgruntled air had left him. He seemed to be enjoying himself. Johnson was exhibiting the symptoms he generally manifested when Dual and his work were discussed. "He told her that Imer's Saturn an' Neptune an' Uranus an' Mars was on the trail of his Mercury and Moon, but that sort of offsettin' that was th' fact that his Venus an' his Jupiter, with a couple of satellites of the latter was mighty friendly, as well as his Sun. That bein' the case, an' a sort of civil warfare havin' developed in Imer's affairs, horoscopically speakin', there's considerable work to be done, which is where Jupiter's satellites come in."

"Talk sense," our visitor growled. "It's Lamb they had before the commission."

"I am talkin' sense," Bryce rejoined. "It ain't my fault if you can't understand. But referrin' to your remarks concernin' ignorance—"

"Jim!" Suddenly Johnson stopped him with a word. His whole bearing altered, became that of a man demanding serious consideration both for himself and the topic under discussion. "See here, boys, maybe he did tell that girl what Jim says, or something like it. I know the way he talks. But what did he say that a man on the street could understand?"

"Little enough," I told him. "He told her to possess herself in faith, and not to be dismayed. I judge that he referred to the findings of the commission as much as anything by the last."

"An' he told her to hope," said Bryce.

"Faith, hope," Johnson repeated, frowning. "What did he mean by it, boys? I know enough about him to know that when he talks in that sort of secretive way he always means somethin' more than he says."

"Frankly, Johnson, we don't know what he meant beyond that there's something funny about this case, something more than appears as yet."

"Crooked?" he challenged me in a word.

"That's merely an assumption," I returned. "But Jim told you what he said about justice and law, and this morning he said that the aid of the law might be invoked."

"But, good Lord!" Johnson breathed deeply. He seemed wholly mystified. "What's crooked about a man's going crazy?"

"We don't know," Jim said. "An' Dual ain't told us yet."

"But you think there is?" Johnson turned toward him.

"Suit yourself. He's as good as told us to hold ourselves ready to get busy when he gives the word." Jim shrugged.

"You?" Johnson stared.

"Sure." Bryce nodded. "You see we're Jupiter's satellites, Moira Mason is Venus, an' maybe you're the Sun; anyway, I gathered that the Sun represented the law, from what he said."

"Me?" Johnson stood up slowly. Once more he drew a deep breath. "Well, then, he does think there's something crooked about this business, an' he knows where to find me if there is. But it's funny." He wrinkled his heavy forehead in a frown of bafflement.

"Yeah. It's as funny as a funeral—or it's apt to be, for some-body, before it's finished," Bryce agreed.

"Faith an' hope, justice an' the law," Johnson rumbled, half, as it seemed, to himself. "Well, so long. I got to be gettin' back to the station."

"So long," Jim returned as our caller moved toward the door. "Funny," he said. "This mornin' you said he was the law, an' then darned if he don't come up here this afternoon, after not havin' showed about the place for months."

"And yet," I said, "haven't you noticed how when Semi takes hold of a matter things always seem to begin to check out?"

Jim gave me a glance under narrowed lids.

"Oh, yes, I've noticed it, son," he said. "I ain't blind, or even as dumb as I talk."

CHAPTER IX

INTO THE DREADED HOUSE

THAT THEN WAS the situation at the end of the day on which Imer Lamb was to become an inmate of that house of invisible bondage—"Drake's Sanatorium," they called it.

IMER LAMB PAROLED, IN
CARE OF HIS BROTHER

It was so the headlines announced the disposition of the case. The story that followed was but a rehash of those that had gone before it, once more stressing the appalling calamity that had befallen one of the leaders in the club and social life of the city, the world of amateur sport. It was a friendly, sympathetic story in the main. From it one gathered that among those who knew him best Imer Lamb had been indeed a favorite—genuine sportsman in the best sense of the word—that many others were grieved at his affliction besides Bo-Peep.

I read the story, and laid it down. And suddenly on impulse I got up. It was between seven and eight. I told my wife I was going out, and left my house. All at once I had decided to go across the city to that house of invisible bondage, and see for myself what it was like, and meet the man who ran it, Drake.

I didn't expect it to do any good. But I could not see where it could do any harm, and I felt an impelling desire to discover for myself, in so far as I could, the exact surroundings into which Imer Lamb, rich man, war hero, pet of society, and idol of amateur sportsmen, had been inducted by his brother George.

I went down to the nearest trolley line and caught a car, and transferred to another that would take me into the Hillcrest section of the city. On the latter I asked the conductor to let me off as near to the Drake Sanatorium as he could.

On alighting, I found myself on a corner, with directions to walk up the hill to my left. I essayed the climb. Presently the houses fell away to make room for what seemed extensive grounds, and I could see a house, its gables outlined against the night sky, its windows points of yellow light among trees.

Before me was an arched gateway with a lettered sign above it. And before the gateway stood a cab. I turned in at the gate along a paved pathway. A figure of a man was before me. He trudged toward the house, sagging under the weight of what seemed a heavy bag; there was something familiar in his gait. I overtook him in a few reaching strides.

"Kingsley?" I said in tentative fashion.

He turned his head.

"Yes sir," he said, as though not sure of my identity, and then, quickly removing a pipe from his mouth: "Ho, hit's Mr. Glace, sir. Good hevenink, sir."

"Here," I offered, "let me help you with that bag."

I put out my hand.

"Ho, no, sir," he refused. "Thinks for Mr. Himer, sir. Hi'm takin' 'em to 'im. My word, hain't it hawful, sir? Strike me, my 'eart bleeds for 'im, hit does. Th' hidiots—th' bloody, bleatin' h'idiots—thinkin' to make 'im well bagain by shuttin' 'im hup hin ha private jail!"

"Well, they couldn't very well let him run at large in his condition," I suggested as we went on toward the house, the bag he refused to let me carry swaying and bumping against his leg.

"Hi know, sir, Hi know," he assented. "But Hi cawn't believe as 'ow 'e's really crazy. Hit hain't natural. But 'e's 'ere, sir, hand Hi'm bringin' 'im 'is bag. Hand 'ere we hare, sir."

We went up some concrete steps to gain a porch. Kingsley knocked out his pipe, put it in his pocket, and punched the button of a bell. We waited.

Presently the door was opened by a woman in the uniform of a nurse.

"Kingsley, Mr. Lamb's man, ma'am," the valet announced himself. "Hi've brought 'is bag."

"Very well—let me have it." The woman extended a hand.

"Hi'll carry hit. Hit's heavy," Kingsley said. "Besides, hi'd like to see Mr. Himer."

"You're the man he attacked, aren't you?" the nurse inquired.

"Yes'm," Kingsley admitted. "But—"

"Then you'd better not see him. Give me the bag."

Again she reached for it.

And Kingsley surrendered it to her.

"Hall right, missie—hall right. No argument. Good night, sir," he said, and turned to trudge down the steps.

The woman turned her eyes to me.

"Let me take it in for you. I suspect it is heavy, and I want to see Dr. Drake," I said.

"What about?" She was little more cordial to me than she had been to Kingsley. Her face and her eyes both impressed me as hard.

"Merely a casual call," I told her, and took the handle of the bag from her relaxing hold and carried it inside.

"If you'll wait here," she said, and went quickly back along a central hallway to a door through which she disappeared.

Then she was back, requesting me to follow to a room where a man sat in a swivel chair, and met my glance across a large, flat-topped mahogany desk. On the top were several glass jars containing what I took to be the powdered leaves of plants of drug value, and a pair of apothecary's scales. As I entered he was scooping the last of a pile of similar appearance from a paper before him into a wide-mouthed jar.

He covered it with a porcelain top, and lifted his eyes.

"Good evening," he said.

"Good evening, Dr. Drake," I replied.

The man was striking in appearance, dark, with an olive skin, a face lengthily oval, a high-bridged nose, a small tip-waxed mustache, and a small triangular goatee, both black. And the eyes that met mine were so dark a brown as to appear black under the light that poured from a shaded globe above the desk.

He nodded and came around the desk. He was slender. There was a dapper something about him, a meticulous quality to his attire. "Yes."

"I am Mr. Glace," I introduced myself.

"Of Glace & Bryce?" He put out a slender, long-fingered hand that, despite the July night, was cool to my answering touch.

"Yes," I assented with a sense of surprise at the readiness of his answer. "You've heard of me then?"

"Oh, yes." He smiled slightly. "Be seated, Mr. Glace."

"May one ask where?" I queried as I took a deeply-cushioned leather chair. The room seemed part den, part office, part work-room, I thought.

"Oh, from several sources," he rejoined still smiling. "More recently from Mr. George Lamb. He tells me you called upon him yesterday afternoon."

That was bringing things to a head with a vengeance. In a way I felt taken aback. Yet on the other hand it made far easier the introduction of the real motive back of my call, a thing I had been wondering just how I was going to introduce. I wondered just what George Lamb had told him, and I, tried to feel him out. "About his brother," I assented. "Poor Imer. He's going to be missed in the world of sport."

"You're a friend of his, Mr. Glace?" he questioned, resuming his seat back of the desk.

"Not personally," I said, deciding I'd get nowhere by masquerading with this man, who struck me as being decidedly alert. "But a very dear friend of his has interested me in his case. She—"

"Miss Mason you mean?" he interrupted. "Naturally what has

happened has been a shock to her, of course. A charming girl, I understand. Did you—er—wish to discuss my latest patient with me, Mr. Glace?"

I nodded. The interview was proving easier than I had hoped, since actually after I had started for Drake's place, I had wondered if I wasn't indulging in a wild-goose chase. "Frankly, I did," I said. "What do you think of his condition? Dr. Simpson seems to think it hopeless, I understand."

"Pooh!" Drake surprised me by his answer. Once more he smiled, lifted his slender hands, and tapped their fingers one against the other.

"What does Simpson know about it? Hopeless nothing. I expect to have the man back to a practical normal before long."

"Real—ly?" I actually stammered. I had expected anything save the man's assurance of Lamb's recovery, I think.

"Absolutely," he almost snapped. "Simpson is like so many of his kind. He considers the disease, and not the patient. One can't generalize in cases of this sort, Mr. Glace, any more than they can in any other disease type. One must study not only the disease, but the man. Lamb is healthy, strong as a lion. Physically he is in the pink of condition. He'll be back trying to break records again before long."

It was amazing. Dual's words came back to my mind. Although in different language, he had said almost the same thing.

"Does that surprise you, Mr. Glace?"

I heard him question, became conscious that I had made no comment on the preceding remark, and hastened to make amends:

"It certainly does surprise me, Dr. Drake, but not unpleasantly, I assure you. It's most encouraging. I wasn't looking for it, however, when I came."

"Probably not," he agreed. "Smoke, Mr. Glace? I can offer you a cigar or a pipe."

"The cigar, then, if you please," I accepted, and as he drew a box from a drawer of the desk, I took one of the thin brown rolls, and set it alight. "You've been engaged in your present line of practice long, have you, Dr. Drake?"

"About four years," he returned, taking a pipe from a tray, and tamping it with tobacco from a jar on the desk. "I practiced in Los Angeles before that."

The conversation having taken a personal turn I asked another question. There was a framed diploma on the wall of the room, but I could not read it from where I sat. "You're a graduate of what school?"

"Waburn College. That's in Missouri." Suddenly he laughed. "And medically speaking, I'm from Missouri, Mr. Glace, in showing asses like Simpson what I mean by medical work. Take this Lamb case for instance. George Lamb came to me yesterday after his brother had been arrested, and Simpson had expressed himself. He told me what had happened, and I gave him my advice.

"That, I think I may say without exactly flattering myself, was the main reason why he went before the commission appointed to dispose of his brother's case with the proposition to have him paroled. I explained to him the essential difference between my methods of handling such cases, and what we might expect anywhere else. There is too much routine in such matters.

"That far, Simpson is right. Homicidal mania is regarded generally as largely hopeless. In the great majority of institutions it would be treated from that standpoint from the first.

"Personally, however, I've discarded the word hopeless from my vocabulary. You'd he surprised how often it's the wrong word to use. Until recently, I admit, mental diseases have been rather hopeless because not well understood, But I'm going to tell you, Mr. Glace, that like any other disease that flesh is heir to, mental diseases in the majority of instances, can he cured. I—" Abruptly he broke off, leaned forward, cocking an ear as it appeared, his hands gripping the edge of the desk.

And then I heard it, too, what I had not heard before, but

what his ear had undoubtedly caught, a woman's scream, faint, far off as it appeared, but high-pitched, shrill, the cry of what seemed a tortured body, a tortured soul. Once it came, and again, somewhere in the farther reaches of the house.

And hard upon it, while Drake still held his listening posture, before he had relaxed, came footfalls, hurrying footsteps in the hall outside the roam where we sat. The door was drawn open, and the woman who had admitted me appeared.

"Doctor—Miss Ashton— She is becoming violent again," she said.

"Very well." Drake nodded in understanding. His glance turned from the nurse to me. "You'll excuse me, Mr. Glace. Glad to have met you. Sorry to have to cut our conversation short, but—"

"Of course," I assented rising.

"Then, good night. Mrs. Porsum will show you out."

Drake hurried from the room, and left me with the woman.

"This way, sir," she said.

"Thanks," I said somewhat dryly. As a matter of fact, I knew my way out.

She trailed me to the front door, however, and I let her close it behind me as I passed through it, and ran down the steps Kingsley had descended some half hour before with the wistful expression his failure to see his master had set upon his face.

I ran down them, and made my way along the concrete path toward the street. My call had amazed me. It had netted me nothing except a personal contact with Drake, and the knowledge that he had practiced medicine in Los Angeles. But it had yielded me through that the positively, almost enthusiastically expressed opinion that Lamb would recover, whether Simpson thought he would or not, that before long he might depart from this House of Invisible Bondage.

I paused as I reached the street; and shuddered as I stood there looking back.

CHAPTER X

SEMI'S METHODS

I WENT DOWN to the corner, and waited for my car. I was in very nearly the mental condition of Johnson when he left our office that afternoon. For the life of me, I couldn't see, as I caught my car and rode along still turning the problem in my brain, where Semi Dual's assertion that justice should he done, and the law take its course, came in. And I couldn't begin to see wherein Dual could make a move.

But I went to see him the next morning. I felt that I should let him know of my call on Drake. And I found him having a late breakfast in his garden, milk, a few beaten cakes, the half of a melon, food he invited me to share. He was always simple in his diet.

But I had breakfasted, and declined the invitation and found a seat. And then I told him what I had done the previous evening, what I had seen and heard.

He listened, sipping at his milk, breaking bits off a cake with his fingers, taking a morsel of melon now and again.

"Dr. Drake said that he felt assured of Lamb's practical recovery," he said when at length I paused. "You are certain that he used the word 'practical,' my friend?"

"Why, yes," I said. "His exact words were 'a practical normal,' but I attached no special importance to it at the time." I frowned. Dual had picked the word out of my narrative in a way that once more excited conjecture in my mind. And immediately he spoke again:

"A human characteristic, Gordon, a human failing at times. Mankind is so often far-sighted that it misses the nearer thing. But at least you remembered the form to repeat it."

"But, Semi, do you assume that he meant Lamb's recovery would he less than complete?" I exclaimed.

He crumbled a bit of cake, moistened it with a sip of milk, and rolled it on his tongue. "One may only assume without knowing what a man has in his mind. At least we may assume that he meant a recovery to a degree to permit of the man's return to the everyday life of man," he returned at length.

Bo-Peep—Moira Mason—that clouded sunbeam of a girl, I had led here to this garden myself—what would a recovery less than complete mean to her?

"But I think that Venus will not he cheated," he said as so often in the past he had read my innermost mind. "That which a woman seeks in purity of heart and purpose, being within the law of life, is a hard thing for even the stars to deny to her who as the Hindu calls her is a Worker in the Workshop of the World." His glance shifted, ran past me toward the door of the tower. "But wait; here comes our friend Henri, with some message, I think."

I turned my head. Henri was approaching. "Master, your friend Bryce rang the telephone but now, and I answered. He says that the young lady who was with you yesterday morning is in his office, and wishes to see you again," he announced.

"Let the maiden come up," Dual directed. Again his eyes met mine. He smiled faintly. "Venus," he said.

I nodded; rose. It was in my mind to withdraw. But Semi lifted a hand. "Sit again, my friend," he checked me. "Wait till we see what Venus brings."

I resumed my seat. Neither of us spoke. We simply waited there beside the little table until the chimes rang softly, and the slender figure of Moira Mason came toward us along the path from the head of the stairs. And then we rose.

"Welcome, Venus," Dual spoke in greeting. "For it comes to me that you come bringing aid."

"Oh, Mr. Dual," she said, "I really hope so. I had to see you, speak to you about something that came to me last night." She was breathing quickly, her eyes were lighted and there was a tinge of heightened color in her cheeks. "You know where they took Imer yesterday, I suppose?"

"Into the House of Invisible Bondage from which he shall come out." Semi inclined his head. "Yes, Venus, I know the place."

She nodded. "I felt sure you would. But last evening I rang up Imer's rooms. I knew his brother had told me that his man was going to take some of his personal belongings out there, his toilet articles and clothes. So I called Joe and asked him how Imer seemed, and he told me they wouldn't let him see him.

"It's"—her lips quivered—"it's as though they were keeping him prisoner. But you know who I am, Mr. Dual. I have money, and I want to use it for him. And I thought that perhaps if I were to employ a private nurse or attendant, it might help. But, of course, I felt that I must seek your opinion first."

As she paused, Semi Dual's gray eyes lighted. There occurred in their depths a phenomenon I had seen before, as though in each had been struck into sudden life a tiny point of fire. It glowed there briefly. And then he smiled. "And did I not just say, and did I not say yesterday morning, that through Venus, aid should come in this matter?" he replied.

"And you have done well in laying this plan before me, since to Jupiter is assigned the place of judge in the galaxy of the stars. Wherefore I say to you, that the thing is well thought of, in so long as you permit Jupiter to select the man in order that the one who assumes this rôle may be one in whom we may place an implicit trust."

I glanced at him, and found once more in his eyes those tiny points of fire; they were like the germs of a purpose, ready to burst into concrete action. It came to me that already that action was taking shape, that this plan Bo-Peep had suggested was one Dual was adapting to his ends, that in it he was even now making a move.

"You know of someone?" I Moira Mason cried. Suddenly she was radiant, a quiver with the carrying out of her suggestion, fired by the determination to put it into force.

"There is a man in my mind," Semi told her. "Fret not concerning the man, my child. Thy part must be to gain the consent of those who at present control the body and mind of the man you love. Wherefore to the end we seek let me suggest that you take our mutual friend, Marya Harding, who is well know to the city's social life, and that, with her, you wait upon your lover's foster brother, George Lamb, and explain what you propose.

"It is not beyond precedent even in a private institution that a private attendant be provided for a case. You, with Marya to aid you, will insist upon your wish. Say to him that you will provide the man, and remunerate him out of your own purse."

"You think he may refuse?" Some of the light went our of Bo-Peep's face.

"He will not refuse Venus, with a friend with her." Again Semi smiled.

And suddenly I laughed. The thing was—well—Dualesque. It was the way in which he so often worked. It carried in it the elements of a subtle finesse. But that was not what excited my laughter.

That was induced by my thought of George Lamb faced by the two women, even should he object to what they had come to propose. Of course that he would object was by no means certain. He might throw himself into cooperation with them if in so doing he thought he would assist that recovery of his brother, which last night Dr. Drake had so positively asserted was a thing practically assured.

But if he did not, if for any reason he was unfavorable to the project, I could picture him battling against it and being beaten, harried into consent by Marya Harding and Bo-Peep. Dual had spoken truly when he said women were hard to refuse; he was a keen psychologist.

"You're delicious." Moira Mason's red lips quirked. They were red this morning. The light came back to her eyes, flashed, steadied to a firm determination. "I'll go get Marya, and we'll drive down and see George, and as soon as it's all arranged I'll telephone Mr. Glace and—"

"My man will be in readiness, with a full understanding of his part," said Semi Dual.

"Then I'll go," Moira declared. "And, thank you—oh, so much. Right now I can't tell you what I feel. But some day Imer and I—"

"Thou and Imer," Dual repeated. "Go, Venus, in faith and steadfastness of purpose, and thou, Friend Glace."

We went down the path to the stairs. The elevator cage came up, and we entered, and I bade her good morning at the seventh floor.

Bryce came in the minute I was in my room. "Hello," he said. "Where you been? Bo-Peep was here awhile ago with somethin' on her mind, and I phoned up, an' Henri told me to let her come through. She's—"

"She's on her way to see George with Marya Harding," I informed him, and went on and put him in touch with what had just occurred as well as what I had done myself, the night before.

"And she's goin' down to interview George now?" he said when I was through. "Trapped kitten, I'd like to listen in on that interview. I'll bet they warp his shingle before they're through. Dual's right as rain. What could any guy in George's place hope to do but kick in when he was faced up by a coupla swell janes?"

"Just the same, Imer's sweet Patootie seems to be one of his pet peeves, an' I bet their buttin' in there with this private attendant proposition is as welcome to him as bad news from home. Even at that he can't be sure what Semi's doin' to him. It's natural; but it's slick."

"Just what do you think Semi's doing to him?" I asked as much to see what he'd say as anything else.

"Huh? Look alive, the undertaker's comin'." He grinned in my face. "You know as well as I do that Dual's gettin' his own man into that place. That's why he insisted on pickin' Imer's he-nurse himself. Nurse, my eye! Lamb needs nursin' the same way a millionaire needs free soup. Semi sees the chance to annex an extra pair of eyes an' ears, an' he ain't passin' it up.

"It's tough on George, but once those two women get into his office he can't do less than accept, without showing a lack of a proper brotherly interest in Imer, whether he likes it or not. It's a squeeze play, son—that's what it is." He chuckled.

His bearing was one of elation, if not actual eagerness. My account of this latest development seemed to have filled him with an anticipation of other impending events. And I had to admit that his deductions seemed logically correct.

"Granting all that," I said, "it would appear that, despite the flivver of your investigations of Acme Film, you are still unconvinced that George really feels what you call a brotherly interest."

"Oh, he feels an interest all right," Jim protested. "I said 'proper' interest. Cain felt an interest in Abel when he hit him with a rock or whatever he is supposed to have used."

"Still," I rejoined, "we must not forget that last night when I visited Drake the man showed an unexpected frankness in discussing Imer's case, or that, according to his story, George apparently took the step calculated to react to his brother's best advantage, on professional advice."

Jim frowned as he weighed my words.

"Well, yes," he assented, pursing his mustache. "Naturally his bein' so dead sure that Imer was goin' to recover was surprisin', but who in Hades is Drake?"

"He's seemingly an enthusiast in his particular line of practice," I returned. "He's a graduate of Waburn College, in Missouri."

"From Missouri, eh? Well, so's a mule," said Bryce. "But that ain't the point. The question is whether Drake knows as much as he'd like folks to believe—as much as he says. Is he the real goods, or just a plausible grafter makin' his way out of the misfortunes of other folks?"

"Your idea being that he persuaded George to let him handle his brother's case, intending to stall it along with fictitious hopes of a recovery as long as it paid," I suggested.

"I don't know what my idea is." Jim scowled. "All I know is that I'm dead sure there's something hidden somewhere in this business, an' that Semi knows it an' is fixin' to dig it out. There's a frame-up in it somewhere, m'son."

"What sort of a frame-up?" I asked. Jim always thought best when he talked out loud.

"I don't know, of course," he grunted. "If I did I wouldn't be sitting here, engagin' in a hemorrhage of words. But, well, did you ever see this here play, 'Blossom Time?' There's a character in that who thinks everything he sees or hears is suspicious. An' I'm in a good deal the same frame of mind myself. What sent Imer off his head? Maybe his goin' balmy, as Kingsley calls it, ain't no more than incidental. There's a lot more than his sanity could be mixed up in this."

"You mean money?" I suggested.

"Money is a mighty potent word," he declared. "But I ain't sayin' it's the one to use. I'm talkin' plenty, but not sayin' much. I guess what I'm doin' really is just followin' the play of Jupiter and Venus. After all, I'm nuthin' but one of them satellites."

"And the tail doesn't wag the dog," I observed.

"Not customarily," said Bryce. "A ship an' a pushcart are two of the few things I know of that steer from behind. Not that the dog needs wagging in the present instance. What I'm grouchin' about is this sittin' around waiting to be wagged. Even if I'm nuthin' but a satellite, I'd like a chance to satellite."

I nodded. I could understand. His attitude was characteristic. He was happy when at work, but idle, waiting for the time to get into action, he was restless and chafed. I felt a good deal the same as he myself. "Well, at least, Dual made what it seems we both feel is apt to prove an important step this morning."

"Yep." Bryce got up. "An' I reckon the thing for us to do, is to wait till he decides to use his satellite instead of his main planet." He took himself off, leaving a blue trail of smoke.

I turned to my desk and tried to fix my attention on my mail, as yet unopened, and on routine work. That kept me fairly well occupied till nearly noon. But just before twelve my telephone rang, and I drew it to me and found myself listening to Moira Mason's voice:

"Mr. Glace? Oh, Mr. Glace, will you please take the trouble of letting Mr. Dual know that it's all fixed? You know I told him I'd telephone you after we'd seen Mr. George Lamb. Mr. Lamb wasn't in favor of my plan at all at first, but Marya and I persuaded him before we left; and he promised to telephone Dr. Drake. You'll let Mr. Dual know?"

"I will, and at once, Miss Mason," I replied.

"You're awfully kind—"

"Not at all."

"Thank you. Good-by." I heard her hang up.

I rose and turned to the other telephone on the wall, and waited until I heard Semi's voice.

I told him what Bo-Peep had said, and waited again through what seemed a long minute before he made response.

"Very well. Henri is out somewhere purchasing a nurse's outfit at present. I shall dispatch him as soon as he returns. In the meantime telephone George Lamb's office, and learn if he is in. If not, inquire if they know where he has gone—but give no name. If they know of his whereabouts, learn it. If he has gone to Drake's place, well and good. If they say they do not know, call the sanatorium and ask for him; but if he answers, do not converse with him. That is all. And please attend to it at once."

I called Lamb's office. He was gone, and had left no word. I broke the connection, and asked for Drake's Sanatorium.

"Dr. Drake?" I questioned, being answered by a masculine voice. And being assured of his identity, went on: "I'm trying to locate Mr. George Lamb. Is he there?"

"Just a moment," Drake said. "Hold the wire." And then: "Someone for you."

There was a pause and then: "Yes, yes, this is Lamb," came in different tones to my ear.

But I did not answer. Instead I slipped the receiver onto the hook, knowing that central would tell him merely that whoever had called him had left the line.

And then I went in search of Jim. My head was filled with a hundred conjectures. Henri, Semi's own man, was going into the House of Invisible Bondage as Imer Lamb's attendant. Dual could trust him absolutely. He would follow to the letter whatever instructions he should give. Filled with such thoughts I suddenly burst in on Bryce.

"Jim," I demanded, "who do you suppose Dual is sending over to Drake's as Lamb's attendant? It's Henri. He told me so in a conversation over the phone just now."

"That settles it!" said Jim. "If he's sending Henri over there he's convinced of just one thing, and that is that there's something crooked about Drake's place!" he roared. "At that rate I reckon we can look for things to start popping before long."

CHAPTER XI

WEARY WAITING

"**I THINK SO,** too, Jim," I agreed, and sat down. "Further-more—" I went on and told him about trying to locate George Lamb, and the result.

He heard me, and an expression of grim satisfaction woke on his face. "He did not telephone," he said, scanning the words as though to give them added force. "He went over there instead. And Semi thought he might, and wanted to prove it. You've let him know he was right?"

"Not yet. I came in here first. But I will now," I told him, and stood up.

I went back to my own room and used the little phone on the wall.

Dual accepted my report without comment, and I sat down and stared blankly out of a window for some time. Like Bryce, I had come where I expected important developments.

But they didn't come. One day followed another after that till the sum of them reached a week. And nothing happened. Bryce speculated and fumed. Mentally I felt baffled, confused. Semi did not call upon us, and gave no sign of any further move.

After the day on which Henri entered the house of invisible bondage as Imer Lamb's attendant apparently all activities ceased. It was as though the entire episode had never been.

And then quite by accident I encountered Moira Mason on the street. She was coming out of a fashionable shop, and we met face to face. Naturally enough I asked for any news of Lamb.

"He's better, much better, Mr. Glace. At least so Dr. Drake says. But—"The flash of her eyes that accompanied the words died out. "I haven't seen him. The doctor thinks I'd better not. In fact, he thinks I shouldn't even see him for a time after he is discharged, as he says he thinks he will be inside a few weeks. So I'm going away, I think."

"You've told Dual about that?" I questioned quickly, more than a little surprised at her words, though of course I could see that perhaps Drake was right in seeking to remove any and all influences by which the nervous system of his patient might be disturbed.

"Not yet," she said. "But I will, of course. I wouldn't think of doing anything right now without asking his advice. But I want to do whatever is best for Imer. Will you arrange an interview with Mr. Dual for me, Mr. Glace, and let me know?"

I promised, bade her good-by, went on to the office, and called Dual and told him what she had said.

"This evening or in the morning," he assented. "And say to her further to come to me in the future as she needs."

I hung up, called the Mason home, and gave her the message, and hung up again with her soft-voiced thanks an echo in my ears. And despite it I frowned. In a way it was like putting up a set of bars. Dual's final words, giving her entree to him without my intervention, some way impressed me in that fashion. Even in that it seemed to me that Bryce and I were shut out. I sat nursing that thought for possibly five minutes before I turned again to the telephone on the wall.

Moira had said she would visit Semi in the morning. I gave him her answer, and again went back to my desk. That single intermediary action had been my only participation in the matter in a week, and even so, I did not know the result until, some four days later, when Bryce, to whom I had mentioned the incident, came into my room one morning with the announcement:

"Well, I see Venus has beat it to the Coast—San Francisco,

San Diego, Los Angeles. I see it in the paper, though as a rule I don't read th' society notes."

"So Semi let her go," I made comment, smiling, since, as it seemed to me, Bryce must have felt about the same way I did, if he had been following the doings of the social world.

"At least he didn't stop her," he grumbled. "See here, son—let's go up there. This job of bein' a satellite is gettin' on my nerves. Of course I don't know much about astronomy—the orbit of Jupiter, for instance—but it's takin' a darned long time to get anywhere. If this is a taste of satelliting, believe me, m'son, I'd rather be a nurse."

I smiled again. I knew as well as he did that he was thinking of Henri, the man Dual had thrust into the house of invisible bondage. And then I stood up. After all, Dual was our friend, and at least it could do no harm to see him.

"All right, Jim," I assented. "Let's go."

We made our way to the roof.

Dual was in his garden, working among his roses with a pair of gloves and pruning-shears. He straightened from his task and smiled.

"Welcome, my friends," he said. "You have shown patience. And patience is a virtue it is well to cultivate. Speaking of cultivation, you find me at a homely task. Yet a rose is like mankind, in a way. That which grows awry must be lopped off."

"The evildoer," I said, thinking I sensed a cryptic quality in his closing words.

"The evildoer—the crooked branch." He nodded slightly, drew off his gloves, and walked to the bench beside the little fountain. "Sit down, my friends. You come as seekers after knowledge. Yet knowledge, like the full-blown beauty of a rose, is a thing of growth. And growth is a building of cell on cell until the finished structure is complete."

"Meanin' you don't know?" Bryce challenged directly, as was his fashion.

"Nay." Dual smiled. "Or not in a completeness sufficient to

enable me to say to the world of man this is this, and this is this—to furnish that concrete evidence of my knowledge which modern man demands."

It was his way. With all his occult methods of arriving at an understanding of a problem, Dual was yet a practical man. Before this he had said to me: "Material proof for material men." And I understood.

But as he paused Bryce put all his bafflement, all his rebellion against the blind progress of the matter thus far, into two words:

"Henri—Bo-Peep?"

"Henri?" Once more Semi smiled. "Henri, friend Bryce, is gathering straws, as a miser, piece by piece, gathers and hoards his gold."

"Straws? What do you mean—straws?" Jim repeated.

"Straws, yes," Dual returned. "For a straw bending before a wind may point the direction of a storm to follow, and a happening in the course of a human affair, though seemingly no more than a straw itself in importance, may portend the bursting of a storm of wrath."

"Wrath?" Bryce pounced on the word like a hungry dog on a bone.

"Wrath," Dual assented. "For he who sows the wind, my friends, shall reap the whirlwind when the time of the harvest is ready, and the measure of his ill deeds runneth over, and the fit grain is winnowed from the chaff."

"Which I ain't denyin' is sound doctrine," Bryce agreed. "But referrin' to these straws Henri has been collectin', is there any of them that would tend to show when this here now storm is due to break?"

"Not yet," Dual said. "But a man's acts may be turned against him, become as stumbling blocks to his feet. And how much more may we not look for a man to stumble who walks blindly, jostling his fellow, trampling upon his rights, along the path of life?"

"Which bein' interpreted might mean that a guy of that sort was apt not only to stumble, but get shoved?" Jim chuckled.

Dual's lips twitched. "Even so, since he it is who jostles his fellows, tramples over or upon them, is it not still his own act which invariably—finally—brings about his stumble?"

"Oh, sure." Bryce nodded. "I get the point. An' referrin' again to Henri an' his gatherin' of straws, I'm hopin' it won't be long till he finds one heavy enough to bust some camel's back. So now that we've disposed of him, what do you know about Bo-Peep?"

"Miss Mason?" said Semi Dual. "There was nothing for her to do here. Here, like ourselves, she could but wait until straw by straw the burden of evil deeds had reached a breaking point.

"Hence, since there was naught for her to accomplish here at present, I added my advice to that of Dr. Drake's, that she absent herself, by a journey, and recommended our Western coast."

"Until after Lamb's turned out of this joint?" Jim demanded.

"Until such time as she is ready to return," Dual replied.

Jim frowned.

"An', say, now, that's funny," he said. "Of course, I don't know anything about Lamb, or medicine, either. Drake may think it's the best thing for him not to see her when he gets out. But if I was in Imer's fix, an' had been engaged to a girl, I'd think it a rather peculiar thing for her to take a trip just about the time I was likely to be turned loose. I reckon I'd be apt to, ask myself if she considered me as a bit too badly damaged to be eligible as a husband, or what."

"As well you might," Dual returned in agreement.

Suddenly his gray eyes turned from Jim to me, seeming to scan our faces in turn, to ask our understanding, that patience he had said was a virtue to cultivate by each and all.

"My friends," he said. "It is true that a man may read a thing after his own fashion, may know a thing in his own soul. Yet wherein shall it profit him in the eyes of other men if he have not the proof in hand to convince them of its truth? Where-fore, until such time as such proof is given to him, must he abide himself in so far as he may in peace, and even in such abiding be must work. Yet in no sense must he be precipitate in thought, or deed, or speech.

"Wherefore, my friends, what can I say to you, save to wait a little longer, as you have waited thus long, till the course of this further bit of man's folly, man's blindness, man's futile attempt to ignore the law, shall be run."

"Oh, well—lookin' at it that way, why, of course," Bryce said all at once. He breathed deeply in the way of one who surrenders, and stood up. "I ain't denyin' I'm puzzled. But if there ain't nothin' to do but wait, we'll wait. Only I'm hopin' that when the right time shows on that clock of fate you're watchin', we'll get a chance to shine in a sort of reflected glory—which from what I know about it is the way a satellite ought to shine." At the last he grinned. "Come along, Gordon, let's go downstairs and resume this waiting game."

Dual spoke again: "It is a wearing service at times. Yet I am doing a little more myself. As friend Bryce puts it, I am watching the Clock in the Skies."

"Just the same," Jim declared once we were back in the office, "I can't seem to quite get hold of Drake's idea in wantn' to get Bo-Peep out of town. Even if I was crazy, which I ain't, or had been, an' had been in a foolish house, it still strikes me that I wouldn't take kindly to the fact of her bein' off on a pleasure journey, what time I got out. I'd sort of feel she ought to be stickin' around.

"Maybe I'm old-fashioned—got old-fashioned ideas about female faithfulness. But I'd sort of want her present—sort of feel we ought to celebrate th' thing together. Of course, Drake may think it better for Imer. I don't say he don't. But still I can't see where seein' her, playin' around with her could be any worse for him than gettin' out an' findin' her gone. Do you know what I'd do if I was in his shoes?"

"Not exactly," I told him. "What?"

"I'd wait till she got home, an' then I'd go see her an' tell her maybe we'd better call all bets off, that the way it looked to be, her beatin' it just before she knew I was goin' to be sprung was a sort of tacit hint that she agreed with me—that a girl was foolish to book up with a bird who had a weak spot in his dome. Dual himself admitted that wasn't exactly foolish. And—"

"And at the same time he told you that he had given her the same advice as Drake," I interrupted.

"Well, yes." He frowned. "An' it's the last thing I'd have expected him to have said. He says I'm right in feelin' my way about it, an' then says he advised her to do the very thing that would make me feel like that. It ain't like him, even though he does have that darned habit of his of sayin' two things at once. Still it might be that.

"Maybe he actually told us something we weren't bright enough to get. Oh, Pip! I reckon the only thing we can do is to take his advice ourselves and wait."

I nodded. "At last you've reached a logical conclusion," I remarked. "The only thing a man can do is to do what he can, as long as he can't do much of anything else."

"Here! Here! Don't you start usin' reverse English," he grinned. He got up and strolled out, leaving me to take up on our renewed waiting alone.

But not for long as it turned out, since though neither Jim nor I knew it then, Dual's assertion that the Clock of the Skies was turning was to receive confirmation sooner than either of us expected after our conversation with him.

The morning ran away. Bryce and I went out for lunch, and returned. It was mid afternoon. And suddenly Bryce came charging into my room along that little corridor that led from his private office to mine.

"Hey! Grab your hat!" he half spoke, half shouted. "Johnson just telephoned. Hell's broke loose at Monk's Hall again. That valet of Lamb's has gone off his dip or somethin', an' mixed it with Doc Drake. Johnson's goin' over there, an' he says we better grab a taxi an' follow him on the jump!"

CHAPTER XII

AT THE SCENE OF THE ATTACK

I SPRANG UP, reaching for my hat almost before I gained my feet.

"Kingsley! Drake!" I gasped.

"Yes. Come on!" Jim Bryce urged once more, getting into motion.

I followed. We charged through the outer office, and out to the bank of elevator cages. Jim jabbed a button savagely. His cigar was clamped fast between his teeth. He was scowling as we waited for a down dropping cage.

Soon we were down, hurrying to the street. There was a taxi stand half a block up. We hurried toward it, found a disengaged machine and threw ourselves into it, calling our directions to the driver, demanding haste.

Then as the taxi shot away from the stand, I sank back on the cushions.

"That's all Johnson told you?" I said.

Jim nodded. "Yes. He didn't have time for more, I guess. Decent of him to think of callin' me at all."

The taxi was fighting its way through the afternoon traffic. At last it emerged from the more congested streets. Its speed quickened and swept us off and out toward the destination our every nerve was straining to reach.

"Funny," I said for lack of any better comment.

"Yeah," Bryce agreed.

The cab slued around a corner, ran for a block, drew into the curb, and stopped! We leaped out. The marble and terra cotta entrance of Monk's Hall was before us. We made our way inside.

The attendant on the desk marked our coming with a watchful eye.

"We're to meet Inspector Johnson here," I said quickly.

He nodded. "Lamb's suite. The boy will show you." He nodded again, this time in the direction of the elevator grille.

We went up. The door of Imer Lamb's suite stood open as we paused outside it. I marked the broad-shouldered bulk of Johnson through it, and went toward him.

He turned at the sound of our steps.

"Oh, hello, boys," he said. "Come in. Coupla friends of mine, doctor."

"I have met Mr. Glace before," Drake acknowledged. He sat on a chair, holding a wadded-up handkerchief to his cheek. As he spoke he removed it, and disclosed the reddened lines of what seemed newly acquired scratches.

So much I saw as I nodded to him, and noted Joe Kingsley stretched out on a couch on the other side of the room with two uniformed members of the police force seemingly on guard.

"What happened?" I asked.

"Drake's been tryin' to tell me," Johnson returned. "I just beat you by a scratch. Accordin' to him, he came up here to see Kingsley, an' the bird attacked him. Go on an' finish your story, doc."

Drake smiled rather grimly. "Perhaps I'd better begin it again, for the benefit of Mr. Glace and his companion, who, I assume, may be Mr. Bryce," he suggested.

"Sure," Johnson assented. "Wait till we sit down." He found himself a seat, and Jim and I followed suit. "All right. Go ahead, doc."

"As I told you before," Drake began, "I came up here to see Kingsley, who is Mr. Imer Lamb, my present patient's man, and the one whom when he became mentally deranged, Mr. Lamb attacked. For reasons of a purely professional nature, I felt that

it would not be well to have Kingsley continue on in the same capacity after Mr. Lamb was released. He—"

"He's goin' to be released?" Johnson interrupted in a tone of what I thought was surprise. Furthermore, I caught his eye, and fancied that it was turned toward me to mark the effect of Drake's announcement.

"Oh, yes," Drake declared. "Mr. Lamb's improvement since he has been in my hands has been consistently toward recovery, as I felt assured it would be at the time I took him in charge."

"You mean he's gettin' well?" This time there could be no doubt that the announcement was totally unexpected on Johnson's part. Simpson had taken the opposite stand, and the inspector fairly snapped the question.

"Oh, yes." Once more Drake smiled. His glance swung to me briefly. "Mr. Glace will tell you that I predicted that the evening of the day after his brother, Mr. George Lamb, brought him to my house. His affliction was of a temporary rather than a permanent type. I expect to release him inside ten days—possibly sooner."

"You think that safe?" Johnson frowned.

"If I did not I would not do it—of course," said Drake. "Of course, such a thing as a relapse might occur. That brings me back to my story, inspector. I felt it best that Kingsley should not continue as his valet for that very reason. He had attacked him once, and well—you can see yourself—there would always be the influence of that, the thought." He spread his slim hands in a gesture.

"So I decided to explain it to the fellow. I stopped, came up, and rang. He admitted me himself. I explained my errand to him, and sought to make plain the advisability of the step. But he took it badly, in a sullen sort of way might describe it best. He said little, just nodded now and then, and mumbled until right at the last when he asked a question; 'You're goin' to run me away, are you? You're goin' to run me away?' he said.

"And when I assured him that I felt sure it would be best, he attacked me. It was so sudden that he took me off my guard. He threw himself on me, but I managed to tear loose and thrust him from me, and you know perhaps that he's more or less a cripple. As I thrust him back he stumbled and went down and struck his head, knocking himself unconscious against the legs of that table there—" He pointed to the bit of furniture in question, a heavy carved table on which were some books, and magazines, and an ornamental tobacco jar.

"Was he injured?" I interjected.

"Nope, I don't think so, though we'll have him looked over," Johnson answered, "He's breathin' all right, though he ain't come out of it yet. I telephoned for an ambulance before you showed up. Doc here says he'll be all right."

"He is probably suffering from a slight brain concussion," Drake explained. "He struck rather hard. Possibly I used more than sufficient force. But a man attacked, gentlemen—one thinks of self-preservation first."

"Oh, don't apologize, doc," Johnson grinned. "I reckon we, any of us, would have done the same if somebody hopped us like that. As it is, he left a few signs of his good intentions on your face. We'll fix him up. Th' question is whether you're goin' any further with it?"

"Preferring a complaint you mean?" Again Drake smiled. "Oh, no. I'd prefer to consider the incident closed so far as my

side of it is concerned. But the man must have what attention
he needs, of course."

"An' he'll get it," Johnson said.

A telephone on a stand on the far side of the room began to
buzz.

"Answer that, will you, Jake."

The latter complied. "The ambulance, inspector," he
announced a moment later.

Johnson nodded. "Thought so; tell 'em to bring a stretcher."

The officer did as he was instructed, and hung up.

Johnson rose. "Well, then, that's all there is to it, I guess," he
said. "I'll have him carted over to the hospital, an' put to bed.
How did he act when he let you in today, doc—any different
from usual?"

"Why, it's hard to say." Drake appeared to weigh his words.
"I'm not acquainted with the fellow, you know. But as I told you,
he appeared sullen, morose; and then, of course, at the last like
a man violently enraged."

Johnson nodded. "Still, you wouldn't say he acted as though
he'd gone foolish, too, would you?"

"Insane, do you mean?" Drake queried quickly. "Well, inspector, his attack partook something of the nature of an acute
emotional insanity, of course. But I fancy that after he recovers
from the bump on his head, you'll find he'll be perfectly sane
within a short time."

"Brainstorm induced by his thinkn' you was takin' his job away,
eh?" Johnson suggested.

"Perhaps," Drake agreed. "You know the man is a war victim,
crippled by his wounds. Sometimes, inspector, a physical injury,
a wracking experience, warps a man's entire nature, and brings
about an unstable nerve balance. Our shell-shock cases are
instances of that."

"Sure," Johnson accepted. "Come in, boys," he called to the
ambulance attendants who paused outside the door of the suite.

They entered with their stretcher; Joe Kingsley was lifted upon it, and carried out. He moaned slightly as he was moved, and opened his lids for a single instant, only to drop them the next.

"Coming out, now, inspector," Drake remarked.

I crossed to stand beside him. "Lamb is nearly recovered then, Dr. Drake?" I asked.

"Remarkably improved, Mr. Glace," he replied.

"That night I called at your place you prophesied that he would return to a 'practical normal,'" I continued. "Does that mean that his recovery is likely to prove—shall we say—an unstable thing, Dr. Drake?"

And again, as when speaking to Johnson, he spread his hands. "I'm not an infallible prophet, Mr. Glace," he returned. "Lamb is practically normal now. Yet it is presumable that should the same conditions as those which first produced his trouble pertain, they might induce the same thing. We can only hope that such conditions will not again occur. If they should not, I feel sure that Mr. Lamb will continue sane. But you can perhaps see the application in that of my determination to see that Kingsley did not stay on as his man, to act as a constant reminder."

"Oh, yes," I said, "I see your point." It was plausible enough. To a physician the end result of his treatment is the main thing. An apparent cure, or even an improvement which does not endure is neither a credit nor a satisfaction to men of the medical profession."

As I spoke, Drake turned to Johnson. "That's all then, inspector? I may be getting on?"

"Oh, sure," Johnson assented. The men with Kingsley had gone. "I'll have 'em lock up these rooms till they get word what to do with them."

"Tell them to call Mr. George Lamb, my patient's brother, you know," Drake offered. "Or I will do it, if you like."

"Sure. Go ahead," Johnson agreed.

"Then, good morning—good morning, Mr. Glace." Drake left the suite.

Johnson eyed his retreating back. "Lamb out of his mind, an' then this bird Kingsley out of his. Funny," he voiced a half thought.

"Their both goin' off their heads in this dump?" Jim caught up what seemed his thread of meaning.

"Yes. That is, if Kingsley is off his head," Johnson said slowly. "I'm goin' to have Simpson look him over. It can't do any harm. An' I'm goin' down an' see if any of the folks around here have noticed anything about him to make 'em think he might be workin' a screw loose the last few days."

"Good thought. Let's hop to it," Bryce urged. His lids were tense at the corners. There was a speculative expression on his face.

We descended to the ground floor, and Johnson questioned the youth on the desk; and the elevator attendant, as two of the operating staff as likely as any others to have noticed anything out of the way in Kingsley's bearing during the past week.

Both agreed that the valet had kept largely to himself, spending most of his time in Lamb's suite, that he had been very quiet in his bearing, speaking seldom to any one unless addressed.

"Looked like he was takin' Lamb's blow-up pretty hard," the deskman said. "He sure was overboard about Lamb. But then, Lamb was pretty good to him, I guess. 'Bout all he's done for days has been mope about his rooms, except when he went out with a bag or something he was takin' over to this place of Drake's."

"Broodin'," Johnson summed it up after we had walked out to where our taxi and a police car waited at the curb. "Broodin' over Lamb, an' waitin' for him to get out. Then Drake comes here with his plan for puttin' the skids under him, an' he blows up."

"Maybe," Jim half-assented. There was still that look of consideration on his face.

"Well, I got to be goin'," Johnson said. "I'll let you know what Simpson thinks after he's had a look at this baby."

"Do," I accepted. "It was good of you to call us. Let us know, too, if Kingsley says anything himself after he wakes up."

We watched him drive off, and entered our own cab. It got under motion, turned, and headed back for the Urania before Jim spoke. Then it was to ask a hypothetical question that he finally used his voice:

"Drake goes up there to tell Kingsley he's goin' to be fired, an' Kingsley jumps him. That's the meat of the story. An' it may be all the meat at that. I'm not sayin' it's not. But here's this: if Drake wanted to wise Kingsley up to the fact that he thought it best for him to clear out after Lamb was well enough to be released, why couldn't he have done it almost any day when Kingsley went over there with things for Imer, instead of comin' down to Monk's Hall on a special trip."

"Why, indeed," I asked myself. When Drake had told his story it had seemed consistent enough. And yet if there was a weak spot in its structure it appeared to me that Bryce had ferreted it out. It hinted at some unexpressed motive other than merely to tell a man that he soon would be out of a job, some other angle in the matter which might have been the real cause of Kingsley's attack. It hinted that Drake's story might be true as far as it went, which was only far enough to cover half the truth.

"Correct, Jim," I made response. "Why did he need to slip the information to Kingsley behind closed doors? Telling Kingsley that he wouldn't be needed after Imer was discharged may have been part of it all right.

"But the question is, was anything like that enough to make the man fly at his throat—unless Kingsley was verging toward a mental unbalance similar to Lamb's—and Drake's visit proved a sort of exploding point? That's possible perhaps. But it's theory pure and simple; that both Lamb and his man should suffer mental breakdowns in the same suite of rooms inside two or three weeks is a rather strange coincidence."

"Meanin' you think Joe is really crazy?" he said frowning.

"Not necessarily, of course," I replied. "We don't know yet. Drake suggests an emotional outburst great enough to rob the man of his sense of responsibility for the time being. He may be right. But I'm glad Johnson is going to have Simpson examine the man's condition, even if he does seem to have missed his bet in Lamb's case."

Bryce nodded. "Yes, and I'm glad you told Johnson to let us know anything Kingsley says when he snaps out of it. It may prove interesting," he said.

The cab slowed, and stopped in front of the Urania. We got out, paid the driver, and turned into the foyer.

"All the way up?" Bryce questioned.

"Of course," I agreed.

CHAPTER XIII

THE WEB OF SEMI DUAL

WE WENT UP. Dual was nowhere in the garden. But the chimes rang to announce our coming, and as we gained the door of the tower his voice reached us from the farther room:

"Enter, my friends."

We followed it to its source, and found him once more seated at his great desk, on which was a litter of paper sheets, covered with astrological figures and computations. As we came upon him, he lifted his eyes. They swept us briefly, marked, no doubt, the expressions of our faces that hinted at the story we were bringing, and spoke again:

"So then, the waiting was not so long as it appeared at the time it was advised? Tell me."

We sat down, and I complied, omitting no detail I could remember of the events at Monk's Hall.

"Simpson will examine the man," he said when I paused.

"Johnson said he would ask him to do so." I nodded.

"Which is equivalent to his request being granted," Semi said, and sat lost for a moment or two it seemed to me in consideration. "I should like to meet this Dr. Simpson, I think," he said again after that. "Whereupon, you my friends, shall help me in bringing such a meeting about. You will gain the ear of Inspector Johnson, and you shall say to him this:

"That in discussing this matter, there is one who says that Joseph Kingsley, valet to Imer Lamb, is not insane in any ordinary sense, that his condition is a temporary matter, a thing of days, no more than that, that with attention, and quiet he will very shortly become his normal self; that he will make it a point to contrive a discussion of Kingsley's condition with Dr. Simpson, and will make this statement to him, will so lead the conversation that Simpson may ask who it is that makes so positive a statement without personal contact with the patient himself.

"Physicians, my friends, are sure of their own opinions, and like other men, they are curious. Shall Simpson question such a declaration as Inspector Johnson asserts has been made, should he question the calling of the man who made it, asking whether he be another physician or no, then shall Inspector Johnson say that he is a physician indeed, though not engaged in practice; that in the present instance he speaks more as a psychologist— that he is a friend—and interested in both the man Kingsley's recent actions, and in Imer Lamb's somewhat parallel case.

"And he may tell him further whatsoever he deems best concerning myself. Should then Simpson express a wish to meet and identify an unknown critic, Johnson may perchance arrange an interview between us. Attend to this at once."

He smiled. Back and behind that smile I saw that his gray eyes once more held each its tiny point of purposeful fire.

I rose. "Hearing is obeying," I said in Oriental fashion.

"Holy smoke!" Bryce erupted, once we were outside. "Curiosity killed a cat! Simpson will be curious, eh? Well, I reckon almost anybody would be curious if they were handed a line like that. Dual's after a meeting with Simpson, but he lets Simpson's curiosity bring it about—lets it look as though he didn't seek it himself. Well, he's a psychologist, all right. But what's he up to now? What does he want to get into touch with Simpson for? What's he got up his sleeve? He's usin' a hold-out in this game if he ever did in his life."

"At least," I said, "he's using an indirect approach. Perhaps he feels he has to. Beyond that, Jim, I don't know, of course. But if Simpson is human he's going to ask who had the temerity to make a diagnosis in Kingsley's case without having seen his patient. And after that if Johnson has any tact at all he can bring the meeting about."

"Oh, it's clever enough," Jim chuckled. "But wait till we give Johnson his instructions. Simpson ain't the only bird who is going to be curious."

Johnson verified the prediction after we had located him at the station, and proffered Dual's request. He stared. More than that, he scowled. "What's the notion?" he demanded. "What's he up to, boys?"

"We don't know, as a matter of fact," I confessed.

"You don't know," Johnson echoed. "Well, I wouldn't wonder if that was the truth. That's the way he works. But I don't make it. I don't get this business at all. Where's there any grounds for action in this matter? Lamb's going to be turned loose in pretty good shape from what Drake says. Kingsley will get off with a few days in hospital, unless Simpson thinks he's worse than it appears Dual does."

"Has he seen him yet?" I interrupted.

"No." He shook his head. "But he will, and when I tell him what you've just spilled, he'll go straight up. I know him. He's a touchy lad when it comes to anything of that sort. He's going to go to the mat with me about one minute after I tell him some-body's been takin' that much interest in a case he has anything to do with.

"Oh, I'm goin' to do it," he grinned, "an' it won't be any trouble for me to lead him up to meetin' the guy who handed out the opinion, I guess. Yep, I'm goin' to do it if for no reason on earth but to see what's back of all this. Dual's got a reason.

"I've worked with him enough to know that there's somethin' more'n I can see if he pulls a stunt of this sort. Psychologist, eh? Well, he sure called the turn on Simpson. You can tell him I'm goin' to the front for him the minute I get the chance."

"Well, that's all we was askin'," Bryce told him, and stood up. "I've a notion he knew you would. You bein' the Sun—other-wise the Law in this affair—you've gotta functuate, when the time for your functionating arrives. This apparently bein' one of the occasions—"

"Oh, dry up," Johnson cut him short. "When you talk you sound like a load of junk. I'm doin' this because he asks me to."

"An' because you want to know what it's all about, as you just admitted," Bryce chuckled.

"Oh, go chase your shadow," Johnson said. But he winked as he caught my eye, none the less.

"Nope," Jim shook his head. He knew Johnson was puzzled by this latest move on the part of Semi Dual, but with his interest fully aroused. "I'm just goin' back an' wait. You know what Semi is doin' in this thing, old top?" He imitated Johnson's voice. " 'No,' he said, 'please tell me.' And I answered: 'Why, Semi's just sayin' to the opposition: 'Take your time; the watch is yours.'

" 'Or, in other words, he's sittin' pretty an' watchin' the little' stars chase themselves. He's like a guy in a blind with a gun, waitin' for th' game to walk into range before he shoots.' An' when I said that, he gave me a glance of admiration, an' he says—"

"I'll give you just about two minutes to get out of here, an' go tell Dual I'm on the job," Johnson rumbled.

"That'll be ninety seconds longer than I need. Come along, son." Jim turned toward the door.

Outside he chuckled again. "What'd I tell you? That bird will bring them two together now if he has to use force."

He was in high good humor, and I nodded. "Oh, yes," I agreed. "And after that—well, I suppose Dual might say that the Clock of the Skies had marked another hour in this business, Jim. At least, this much is certain. He wants to meet Simpson, because he has an idea that there is some way in which Simpson may prove of use."

"I guess even a child could dope that out," he returned, "The question that's botherin' me is what way he thinks he can be used."

"Well," I said, "you yourself likened his actions to those of a hunter in a blind waiting for his game to come into range, and sometimes I understand such hunters use beaters to drive their game up in front of the guns."

"Huh?" Jim paused in his stride. "By golly, son, that's an idea," he declared, "but I can't see how it works. I—excuse me—"

We were standing in front of one of the larger shops as it happened, and in the midst of the late shopping crowd. As he uttered the last words in a half-exclamatory tone, Bryce drew back to avoid the slender, modishly-gowned figure of a woman who was making her way toward a town car drawn up beside the curb.

And in the next moment he spoke again: "Miss Norton!"

"Well?" With her hand on the door of the car, the woman paused, and turned halfway as Jim strolled toward her. Her eyes met his without any sign of recognition. Her eyelids flickered, her reddened lips set. Her whole bearing was what one might have expected it to be in a woman accosted by a total stranger on the street.

And Bryce appeared to understand, because he smiled as he again addressed her.

"Oh, don't get upstage because I'm speakin' to you without an introduction, Nathalie, please. I'm just a private plainclothes dick, and I used to be on the force. So it won't get you a thing to make a holler. How's George?"

"George?" she repeated, frowning in a way that knit her delicately plucked brows.

"Sure. George Lamb," Bryce countered. "How'd he take Kingsley's blowin' up this afternoon an' tryin' to spoil Doc Drake's beauty."

"Joe!" Nathalie Norton exclaimed, and caught herself up, biting her lips. "See here, what do you mean by stopping me and asking me such questions—you—you—"

"Name's Bryce," Jim interrupted. "As to why, I just wanted to see if George had told you. Probably will, though, the next time he sees you—tonight or tomorrow. You see, Joe, as you call him, went off his dip, a good deal like Imer did."

"Was—was Dr. Drake hurt?" Suddenly I saw the girl's hand tighten on the handle of the door till the knuckles stretched tight the skin of her glove. Under her rouge her face paled a bit.

"Hurt?" Jim's lids narrowed, though he grinned. "Oh, no. Joe's a cripple. All he did was to get home with a few wicked fingernail scratches. Then Drake knocked him for a row of soup tureens, an' Joe dented the leg of a table with his head. I saw Drake after it was over, an' he went off on his own power, all right. I thought George might have slipped you the news."

"Why?" Abruptly she fought back to her shaken control. "Why are you doing this, really, Mr. Bryce? Why should George Lamb have told me anything about it? Why do you stop me on the street to ask if he has? By what right—"

"Oh, be yourself, Nathalie." Jim shrugged, and smiled as he looked her in the eyes.

For a moment their glances held, and then Nathalie Norton wrenched open the door of her car, and flashed inside. It drew out into the stream of traffic, leaving him standing there on the curb.

"And now what in Heaven's name made you pull that sort of play?" I demanded as he turned back.

"You did, I reckon, m'son," he informed me.

"I?" I said. I didn't comprehend.

"Sure." He nodded. "What you said about hunters usin' beaters to flush their game. She's George's girl, an' she'll tell him about it, of course."

"You know as well as I do, that women like her have expensive tastes. Notice how she was dressed, the make of car she drives?"

"George makes a lot of money, an' he handles Imer's end of the estate. I don't know nuthin', but girls like that cost a lot to court; an' George as good as told us Imer knew nothin' about the business that day we was down there. George seems to do about as he likes. That way the question might be is Imer as well off as he thinks—or thought he was?"

"Still harping on that string, are you?" I asked.

And again he nodded. "I'm apt to try harpin' on anything that's got a string right at present," he declared.

"Your idea, then, is that George may have been looting Imer's end of the estate?" I suggested.

"Well, such things have happened," he scowled. "But my main idea in speakin' to Nathalie was that she's close enough to George to tell him, an' the more burrs you put under a saddle the more apt a mule is to jump."

"Oh, I understand that," I assented. "But did you notice the way she acted when you mentioned Drake?"

"Did I?" he rejoined. "I'll say I did. And that's another thing. Why should she? Why should the idea that Drake might have got hurt make her turn white? I don't know the answer, son, but there is an answer. Which reminds me that we've got one for Dual before we can call it a day an' knock off work. An' I reckon I've got a confession to make. Let's get along and get it over with."

We turned back into the sidewalk traffic, made our way to the Urania, and for the second time that afternoon we ascended to the roof.

Dual sat as before in the inner room of the tower, still busy with his charts.

We told him the result of our errand; and then Jim described our meeting with Miss Morton.

"This but matches a missing piece of the picture." Semi said at the last. "Your impulsive action should do no harm, I think."

"Well, I'm glad it matches." Jim glanced at the symbol-marked sheets of paper on the desk. "You've been watchin' that clock you was speakin' about this morning?"

"The clock of the skies," Dual returned. "Ah, yes. In a sense I have been watching it, friend Bryce, and in another sense I have been weaving a web."

"Web?" Bryce repeated. "What sort of a web?"

"A web of invisible threads—selfishness, cupidity, lust, duplicity, false pretenses, treachery, callousness, greed—things that snare the feet of man and hold him prisoner to his baser elements, things by which the feet of the one who is guilty of them may be snared, when the entangling maze of their destroying manifestation shall be thrown about him, and he finds himself enmeshed like even to a helpless fly which has blundered blindly into a spider's web."

My mind reached out for his meaning. Days before he had spoken of soul elements, naming faith, hope, love. He had spoken, too, of a harvest of wrath to be garnered once it had been raised from the seed of men's deeds. He had spoken of law and justice, and of a time when what was to be, would be. And now he was speaking of a web—he had said he was weaving it.

"Semi, you mean that this web is your estimate of this whole affair, the elements that have led to it, that point toward its termination, that it is such threads as you have named that in the end are going to grip and hold the ones who have used them toward the accomplishment of whatever they were striving to accomplish fast?"

"Unless I have woven my web all wrong," he said, and smiled back into my questioning eyes. "You are right; that to which I referred as a web is, as you put it, my estimate of this matter, its activating elements, its foreshadowed termination.

"Consideration for the rights of others, truthfulness, decency, fair dealing, integrity, human kindness—those things endure, exalt the soul of man rather than drag it down. The spider tints its web with iridescence, makes of it a tinsel thing to lure its victim. And who would knowingly accept tinsel for gold?

"The true Path of Attainment is not crooked. It does not deviate, or twist, or turn. It is a straight and narrow path cut through a morass of error. Unhappy is he who steps aside—in the end. And there are so many, so many, who struggle futilely in the mire, caught, tangled in the web of their own self-blinded desires."

It wasn't a pleasant picture he painted in words. I thought of the girl Bryce had spoken to this afternoon. She was beautiful in her way, attractive, young. But she was caught in a web of tinsel. It glittered—that web that held her, but it was dragging her down.

Here again I thought was another type of invisible bondage—wherein one was caught and held by a web of invisible threads, a self-made web, woven out of the things one had done one's self.

And Dual in his own peculiar, uncanny fashion, was using those very things to confound whoever it was he thought amenable to justice, whoever it was against whom he had said the law should take its course in this affair of Imer Lamb. Here high up in his tower, he sat and spun his web of invisible threads to trap them; or rather he was letting them spin the threads, and then gathering them into his strange, capable hands.

Not as a spider was he spinning. Rather he was Jupiter, the arbiter, the judge as he had named himself in the beginning, watching, waiting, marking the puppet play of those he watched.

I stood up. "Well," I said, "Johnson will doubtless let us know when he has managed to contrive a meeting with Simpson. When he does, we'll get word to you at once."

"Do so," Semi accepted. "The meeting will be contrived past any doubt. When one works with human elements of a known value, one may safely predicate results."

"And that's psychology," Bryce grinned as he rose.

"A practical application of psychology, friend Bryce," Dual assented. "The psychologist, like the chemist who blends two known reagents, may feel fairly well assured of how they will react."

CHAPTER XIV

SEMI VISITS JOE

IS MONK'S HALL HAUNTED?

IT WAS SO they ran the story of Joe Kingsley's assault on Drake on the local page the morning after it had occurred. But outside the suggestion of the caption, they gave it little space, beyond what was essential to a narration of the salient facts. Joseph Kingsley, valet of Imer Lamb, who some weeks before had been the victim of an assault at the hands of his master, had yesterday in a measure duplicated the attack on the person of Dr. Drake, head of Drake's Sanatorium, where Lamb was now a patient. The attack had occurred in Lamb's suite in the fashionable apartment house.

I read the story, and laid it aside. It gave me the information that Simpson had not gone into the matter of Kingsley's mental condition as yet. The caption impressed me as being in very bad taste. From what I knew of such things, I felt assured that whoever wrote it would have a chance to sweat. Monk's Hall would hardly fail to register a protest through its management against a thing so apt to attract unfavorable attention, I thought.

I went to the office, and took up routine work. I had neglected it the day before, and it held my attention to the exclusion of pretty much everything else, for a couple of hours.

Then Johnson showed up. "Kingsley woke up this mornin'," he announced. "An' outside a sore head he seems pretty much all right."

"Wait a minute; Jim would rather get this first hand," I requested, and punched a buzzer to summon Bryce.

Johnson waited until Jim appeared, and then resumed.

"As I told you, Kingsley seems about himself this mornin', except that he acts a little dazed, an' swears he don't remember a thing, after Drake told him he was goin' to be fired out of a soft job."

"He remembers that far though, does he?" I asked.

"Oh, yes." Johnson nodded. "His story and Drake's match pretty much. He says the doc came in, and asked him for some tobacco Lamb left there when he was carted off to the sanatorium—an' he gave it to him. Then he says Drake told him he wouldn't be needed any longer after Lamb was turned loose. After that, though he claims to have lost his memory till he woke up in the hospital, an' wanted to know what it was all about. That's Simpson's story."

"You've seen Simpson then?" I inquired.

"Seen him! Oh, yes, I've seen him." He grinned. "Him an' me had quite a talk. That's what brought me up here this mornin'. I told you he'd want to know who in time was buttin' in, an' he did. So I told him what you said about Dual's bein' a psychologist, an' knowin' what he was talkin' about.

"That got his interest, an' I took th' opportunity to elaborate— told him I knew him pretty well an' had worked with him on more than one funny case. That cooled him off a bit. An' now he wants to meet him himself. I put it over. Simpson is goin' to give Kingsley the up an' down again this afternoon, an' I've got his invitation for Dual to meet him at the station and go on to the county hospital at two o'clock."

"And that's that," said Bryce. "You told him what Semi said about Kingsley's not bein' crazy, of course."

"Of course." Once more Johnson nodded. "That was what blew him up at first, an' just about doubled his interest after we had had our talk. You better slip Dual the word. I'll be over there an' make the introduction."

I told him I would see that Semi was informed, and he left. Then I used the telephone on the wall, and Dual answered. I told him what Johnson had said.

"Very well," he accepted. "At two o'clock. You will accompany me to the station if you can make it convenient, Gordon. Come to me just before two."

I assented, and a little after half past one I made my way to the roof.

Dual awaited me in the garden, but no longer in his white and purple robes. Today he had laid them aside for the habiliments of a man of the modern world, striped trousers, an English cutaway coat, a silk hat, which to my first glance seemed to add to the commanding quality of his figure, itself above the average height. Varnished shoes and a slender cane completed his costume. All in all his appearance was one to attract the attention of any one we met.

"Welcome, my friend," he said. "It is time that we set out. One should be punctual at an appointment." He fell into step beside me, moving toward the head of the stairs.

We went down them, waited for a cage, dropped down to the street, and entered a taxi at the stand where Bryce and I had obtained ours the day before. We were at the police station within five minutes.

There Dual and Dr. Simpson met. Johnson engineered the meeting as he had said he would. Simpson, as it seemed to me, was the antithesis of Dual—with a rough and ready manner in both speech and dress that but accentuated Semi's elegance.

"Hear you're interested in my cases, Mr. Dual, or should I say, doctor?" he said as Dual and he shook hands, and I saw his eyes quickly sweep Semi from head to foot.

"Whichever you prefer, Dr. Simpson," Dual returned. "I am, as it chances, either or both. But the title matters little save as a means of address, since, after all, our mutual interest is, I think, in the man himself. As to your cases, I have ventured to express an opinion in both. My interest, however, is humanitarian as well as scientific."

"Humanitarian?" Simpson repeated. Both Semi's bearing and his manner of speaking were impressing him, I thought. "I'm afraid I don't just get you, doctor."

"Humanitarian," said Semi Dual, "in as much as anything which affects the welfare or happiness of the individual should excite our interest."

"Oh, yes, yes; that, of course," Dr. Simpson assented. He looked at his watch. "Well, shall we be going? I want to see this chap and get back."

"At your pleasure." Semi slightly inclined his silk-hatted head.

"Then, I've a car outside," Simpson suggested.

The two men passed out of the detectives' room, where their meeting had occurred, and left Johnson and me together. We were not invited to accompany them on their visit to Joseph Kingsley. We were simply left. And there was no reason really why we should have been asked to go along, but in bringing me to the station, and in leaving me there with Johnson after he had arranged the meeting, I fancied I saw but another touch of Semi's infinite tact.

As they disappeared, Johnson threw himself into a chair at his desk, and laughed shortly. He drew out a handkerchief, and wiped his face. "And there you are," he declared. "He comes down here dressed for an afternoon reception, an' as cool as ice, an' I'm sweatin' like a horse. Honestly, Glace, I can't ever make him. And I sure can't make him in this.

"The way he's actin' you'd think he was expectin' to raise merry hell with somebody one of these days. An', for the life of me, I can't see why he should. Drake says Lamb is pretty near well, an' from all I know, his goin' nutty was what started all this fuss. If he gets well—"

"He'll get well," I assured him.

"Dual tell you?" he countered.

And I nodded. "Yes."

"Well, then what's all the fuss about?" he demanded.

"I don't know, Johnson," I confessed. "But you know he said justice was going to be done, and last night he told Bryce and me that he was weaving a web. By that I feel he meant he was gathering evidence."

"Evidence against whom?" He frowned. "Damn it all, who is it he's after, Glace?"

"If I really knew, I think I'd tell you, Johnson," I rejoined. "But I don't. Still, it's my notion that he wanted to meet Simpson, because he thinks he can dig up something he's after better than any one else."

"In his official capacity, you mean?" he queried.

"Official, or professional, or both," I told him. "I don't know. It's a guess."

"Humph!" he grunted. "But you may be right. You know him better than I do, and I know he's a mighty closemouthed party until he's willing to speak. Well, I've done my part in bringin' 'em together, an' if he convinces Simpson there's anything he ought to do, he'll do it. He's a straight shooter all right."

I left him and made my way back to the office on foot. And as I walked, once more I reviewed the entire affair, which, so far at least as Semi Dual, and Bryce, and I were concerned, had begun with the coming of Moira Mason to our office—which had led Imer Lamb into the House of Invisible Bondage, that house on a hill which, despite its high outlook, was but a refuge of sorts for men and women of clouded minds; and ever since had run out a practically invisible course.

The little phone box buzzed again that evening, close to five. Its whirring meant that Semi Dual was back from his visit with Simpson, and was calling for me. I rose and answered.

"Yes. Glace speaking."

"Listen, Gordon, my friend," his voice came back. "Tonight at nine o'clock, you and Bryce will go to the lounge of the Glen Arms Hotel. There you will meet Mrs. Marya Harding, and escort her to the roof. You will remain there at a table, enjoying the evening's entertainment, until the lady expresses a desire to leave.

"You will then drive with her in her machine to the rear of the block in which the Drake Sanatorium is located, stopping opposite a small tradesmen's door in the wall that surrounds the sanatorium grounds in the rear. This gate is customarily locked at night. But a key has been provided for the use of the one who will need it.

"At this gate you will wait until one comes through it, and enters your car. As soon as that one is inside, you will accompany Mrs. Harding to her home on Park Drive. Do you comprehend me fully?"

"Yes, yes," I assured him, startled, filled with vague speculations by this call upon myself and Bryce. "But, Semi—"

"Not now." He halted the question that was rising to my lips. "Attend to this without fail. On it hangs a human life. Afterward all will be explained, or will explain itself."

"We'll attend to it, of course," I promised, and hung up.

A human life, the life of someone in the House of Invisible Bondage, of that someone who would come through the little tradesmen's gate in the rear wall. Was it Imer Lamb? My every nerve was tense as I went in search of Bryce, and found him with his usual black cigar between his teeth.

I told him, and he took the weed from his mouth and stared. "By Heaven!" he said, and stood up. We stood there facing one another through several heartbeats. "They're goin' to try to bump him off?" he went on then in a tone of utter bewilderment. "But that ain't possible, Glace. Drake said he was goin' to be released. Told you, an' me, an' Johnson. They wouldn't dare—after that."

"I don't know. It doesn't seem plausible," I agreed. "But if it isn't Imer, who else?"

"Say," he began with a sagging law, and then he pulled it up, "what sort of a dump, is that place of Drake's?" And abruptly his lids slitted, and he spoke again a single word. "Henri!"

Henri, Semi's own man who, he had said, was gathering

straws. If there were too many straws for him to gather, and they knew he had done it, his life might be in danger, I thought.

Jim put his cigar back again between his lips. "But this here get-away seems to be pretty well planned. We're to meet Marya at the Glen Arms, and go to the roof show. The question is do I go as I am, or wear soup and fish?"

"I think we go as we are," I decided. "I'll meet you at the Glen Arms about eight forty-five."

"All right. I'll be there before you," he said.

And he was, seated on a divan in the lounge, with a watchful eye that lighted as I approached.

It lighted again as Marya Harding came toward us a minute or two before nine, and we rose to meet her, and escort her to the roof, where were tables, lights, music, and a summer roof-garden show. And well might any man's eyes light at sight of her, I thought. She was in a summer evening costume that accentu-ated her darkly Oriental beauty, with a light embroidered scarf of some filmy tissue about her shoulders and throat.

"Ah, here you are, my friends," she said, as she reached us, and extended a hand to each. Her eyes were sparkling, and there was a smile on her red lips. "Bob's out of town, and so, when our other friend asked me to lend him my car and myself this evening, he had to furnish me an escort, and lent me you gentlemen."

"After all, as you may recall, he characterized us as his satel-lites, in the beginning of this muddle. And, it seems, there are really three of us this evening," I responded. "You know, the Persians refer to a beautiful woman as a full moon."

"That's very nice." She nodded, her smile once more flashing out. "Shall we go up?"

The Glen Arms was the best hotel our city boasted, and in the summer was a popular, evening resort. The result was that even so early we found the roof garden thronged. But Marya Hard-ing was well known. A captain bowed before her, and led us to a little table already reserved, well off to one side.

"I telephoned for this in time to be sure we'd get about what we wanted," she said as we sat down. "When our friend asked me to take a hand on behalf of this girl—"

"Girl?" Jim echoed sharply, and as quickly shut himself off. His expression was one of blank amazement.

Marya eyed him. His lips twitched in what seemed to me a faint amusement. "Why, yes. Didn't you know? Didn't you really know?" she said.

CHAPTER XV

THE RESCUE

"NOPE." JIM FUMBLED for a cigar and set it alight. About us at other tables men were smoking. "It's a girl then, is it?"

"Yes." Marya narrowed her lids. "He didn't tell you?"

"Merely the salient details of what we were to do—nothing specific," I informed her.

And suddenly she laughed. "It's his way, isn't it?" she observed. "But with me he was more specific, as you put it, Mr. Glace. It's rather dreadful. I used to know her as a matter of fact.

"She was one of the younger set, a dear girl; I remember when she went to pieces. It was after her mother died. She—her mother, I mean—was an invalid for years. And Gladys—this girl—took care of her pretty much at the last.

"Of course, there were nurses, but there's such a lot nurses can't do, and those things Gladys did. She broke down completely after her mother's death—too much nerve strain, they said at the time. That was over a year ago, and she's been in this place ever since."

Jim stared straight into her face. "Because?"

"I can't tell you here. And I told you it was dreadful, and it is. It's like a horrid story. One hates to think such things could happen, even he planned. It's like a nightmare."

"S-D told you?" Jim asked.

"Part of it. What I told you about her before I knew myself. But he told me why he asked what he did. Please don't look so serious. We're supposed to be a pleasure party by any one who sees us."

"You heard from Miss Mason?" I asked.

"Yes," she answered, once more smiling. "She was in Los Angeles the last time she wrote, but expects to be back in ten days or two weeks."

Here was additional news. This glowing woman seemed to actually know more about certain phases of the matter than either Jim or I. I laughed. "At least we knew she was on the West Coast," I said.

"And why?" she challenged.

I shook my head.

Her brown eyes danced. "I think Bo-Peep was right. Our dear friend is delicious," she declared, and began beating time with a hand to the music. "Mr. Glace, do you dance?"

I rose, and followed her to the floor, where numerous couples revolved; and we spun off through and among its revolving life. "I'm thrilled—positively thrilled by this night's adventure," she confessed. "I feel like a character out of some awfully exciting book."

"You know that a human life depends on its success?" I whispered.

"Oh, then—you do know something?" she whispered back. "Yes, I know. But we're going to succeed, Mr. Glace. Henri, his own man, has arranged everything, of course."

The music ceased. I led her back to the table where Jim sat and smoked. Our refreshments were served. Time ran away in music, dance, and talk. Finally Marya balanced at a tiny watch on her wrist. "I think we had better be going," she suggested.

It was half past eleven o'clock.

We rose and left our table, and made our way down to the street. Marya's car—a closed machine—was waiting in a parking place. We entered, Marya taking her place in the driver's seat.

After a bit we began to climb up a street illuminated only by corner arcs. And at the crest of that street we turned, and ran a block, and turned again, and dropped silently down the slope, the motor cut down to a whisper, literally coasting to a final standstill beside the curb, midway between the intersecting streets.

Beyond us was a wall with an arched doorway, now closed. Above the wall were the shadowy tops of trees against a night sky. There was no moon.

Marya shut off the lights. In the following starlight her face showed white. Beyond those trees was the House of Invisible Bondage, made quite invisible by them, and the night.

We waited. No one spoke. There was a little breeze; it rustled ghostlike in the leaves beyond the wall. I heard the woman beside me catch her breath, and felt I knew what she was thinking. Would she succeed in escaping?—the girl for whom we waited.

Would Henri's plans—Dual's plans—carry? Suddenly the tension that held me relaxed. I breathed more freely. Dual's plans! When had I known them to fail? I stiffened again suddenly. Again Marya Harding caught her breath. Behind us I heard Jim move, and the sigh of the car door opening.

There had been a click of metal, faint, short, sharp like the click of the wards of a lock. And now the little door in the wall was swinging open, and a darkly muffled figure was slipping through. It passed the door and paused, and appeared to stoop. Again came the metallic clicking. And then the slim dark shape was coming toward us, a flitting shadow in the midnight dusk of the street.

It reached us. The car sagged slightly as its weight was lifted to the step; then the door closed softly. Marya released her brakes; with the slope of the street to aid us, we rolled soundlessly forward, one, two, three blocks. Then, as the grade lessened, she let in the clutch. She had left her gears engaged, and instantly the engine purred. She turned, and swung off and away in the direction of Park Drive. I heard her whispering—whispering to herself: "Thank Heaven!"

The thing was accomplished; a vast elation filled me. Out of the House of Invisible Bondage we had brought a human soul! Behind me I could hear Bryce speaking softly, and a softly replying voice. The purr of the engine heightened. We fled through the streets at the limit of legal speed. And suddenly Marya Harding laughed. "Yoiks! Gone away! Are you all right, Gladys?" she called.

"Marya—it's Marya Harding" a girl's voice exclaimed.

"Yes, my child." Once more Marya laughed with a note of nervous tension in the sound of it, as she drove. The car slued around a corner. We were on Park Drive itself. And then we were turning from it into a driveway that led back to a garage. We slid into it. The sound of the motor died. "And here we are," she said. "All out."

We got out. Jim and I closed the doors. We followed a cement walk to a side door, and entered the house. The girl walked with Marya; they were whispering together. Then, as the door closed, the lights struck upon us. Marya slipped the dark coat from her companion, and turned her toward us.

"Mr. Glace and Mr. Bryce, let me present Miss Gladys Ashton," she said.

Ashton! The name struck a memory in my brain of the night I had visited Drake in the House of Invisible Bondage, of the nurse, and the woman, who had come to the door of his study. "Doctor—Miss Ashton. She is growing violent again," she had said. Ashton—Gladys Ashton.

She was a slim blonde, with wide, dark-circled eyes in a drawn, yet now hope-lighted face. She was the girl whose scream I had heard that night, that scream at the recollection of which I had shuddered as I had looked back at the house that held her, that house on the hill, with its windows barred. And now she stood here with a half uncertain smile struggling into being on her lips.

"I am happy to meet Miss Ashton," I faltered.

Bryce ducked his head.

Marya Harding laughed again. "Our friends were good

enough to act as my escort tonight at the behest of the man who helped Henri arrange everything," she explained.

"The man whom Henri calls the Master?" Gladys Ashton questioned. "You know, it seems odd, but so much that is strange has happened to me that nothing seems really odd any longer, he read my horoscope after Henri had asked me the date of my birth.

"And after that he sent me a little saw by Henri; and I sawed the bars, and used soap and the iron filings to hide the traces of my work. And Henri gave me a key to that door in the wall, and told me to use it tonight. Oh, Marya, is it really true; am I really free?"

Marya slipped an arm about her. "Not only free, but safe," she said.

"But you must sit down," she went on. "Come, you shall talk a bit if you wish; and then you must go to bed, and get a good resting sleep."

She led the way into a room I had been in more than once before, a room where I had seen her, herself fighting against what seemed the damning circumstances of an unkind fate. We sat down, Marya attending to seating Gladys Ashton herself.

"And now—if you want to tell us—just a little of all that's happened, we'd like to hear I'm sure," she suggested. "Don't if you'd rather not."

"I—I guess I'd like to," Gladys Ashton said slowly. "It all started after mother died. I broke down. Nerves, the doctors said. And there was so much to be done. You know she left a large estate. That's what started it. Did you know that Mr. John Parkins was mother's brother, Marya, dear?"

"No." Marya shook her head.

"Parkins of the Parkins-Mahlberg Trust Company?" Bryce asked.

Gladys Ashton nodded. "Yes. He came to me and offered to tend to everything—mother left everything to me, you see. But he was very nice, and I was so very tired and I didn't know anything about such matters myself. So I gave him a—a paper to enable him to handle the property, and money—"

"A power of attorney?" I suggested; and glanced at Bryce. He was frowning slightly.

"I think that's what they called it," Miss Ashton replied. "Anyway I signed it, and then he said I ought to go somewhere for a rest and he brought Dr. Drake to see me; and they took me to his place. And I haven't left it since, till tonight.

"I couldn't. They kept me, wouldn't let me leave. I've been a prisoner. They gave me something—I don't know what—something with a hypodermic needle that drove me almost mad, made me say things, and think strange thoughts.

"That wasn't all the time, but only when I grew nearly frantic at the position in which I found myself; I did that sometimes, when I grew almost mad with thinking how I had been tricked, and how powerless I was to help myself.

"They wouldn't let me see any one—gave it out to all my friends that I wasn't myself. Oh, they were clever; they wouldn't let any one see me unless I was drugged. And sometimes, when there were visitors, they would give me the drug, and I'd rave; I couldn't help myself. I—I—oh—Marya." She broke off, fighting for control.

A House of Bondage—a nightmare! It had been both, an invisible bondage, and a long, long nightmare from which she had now escaped.

"But see here," Bryce broke the silence that followed her emotion—engendered pause. "Were you ever examined as to your bein' sane, or insane—I mean by a board of doctors, or anything of the sort?"

"Why, no, sir," Gladys Ashton told him knitting her brows in what seemed an effort of thought. "At least, I can't remember."

Jim glanced at me. "All right. Go on," he said.

"That's about all, I think." The girl resumed her story. "It just went on like' that, Sometimes for days, if I kept quiet, they let me alone. Then when it seemed to me I couldn't stand it any longer, they'd give me that drug, whatever it was. And sometimes after that they would keep me under it for days. It always affected me the same way inside a few minutes after they had injected it."

"Good Lord!" I didn't speak the words, but I uttered them in my thought. The night I had been there she had screamed, and grown violent. The woman Drake had called Mrs. Porsum had come and called him when Gladys Ashton had screamed. The thing was horrible, and excited a sense of revolt as I listened to her further words.

"So after a bit I just began to keep as quiet as I could so they wouldn't give me the drug. And then, Mr. Imer Lamb was brought there, and a man came with him to be his nurse. You know who it was, Marya, of course. His name was Henri, but he was the first one whom I had found a chance to talk to since I had been in that dreadful house, to explain to.

"And he listened, and I thought he believed. And he did; and he did everything else. He told the man he calls the Master—the man who reads people's fate in the stars. And then I began to hope. He brought me the little saw, and gave me the key he had, had made for me from a wax impression he had managed to make of the lock on that door, the key I used tonight.

"I used the saw at night and hid it in the daytime. And you know the rest. And now I'm here with you; and you say I'm safe. And I'm not crazy; I'm not crazy!" At the end her voice shot suddenly up in a passion of protestation.

"Of course you're not," Marya declared, crossing quickly to her and laying a hand on her shoulder. "You're just tired, just all unstrung—worn out. And I'm going to put you to bed."

"I'm not sleepy, though, Marya dear." Gladys Ashton forced a smile to her lips. "I'm too happy—too happy. It's so wonderful to be back in the world again, out of that house."

"I suppose," Bryce spoke again with his sometimes almost brutal directness, "that all the time you've been there, this precious uncle of yours has been playin' ducks and drakes with your estate?"

"I—oh, I don't know." Miss Ashton turned her eyes toward him. "But I'm afraid you're right. He was mother's brother. I suppose be thought he had some right to what she had left.

"I've thought about it, of course. I don't know what he's done, but I've wondered. He must have paid Dr. Drake to keep me there as he did—and he would have had a reason for that. And he was always a speculator. I know it worried mother. He used to come to her for help at times when she was still alive."

"An' durin' the last year, then, he's probably been helpin' himself," Jim rumbled, with a disgusted note in his voice. "Well, Miss Ashton, I'm sure glad to have had even my little finger in assistin' at this get-away of yours, and if there is any way I can help you further—say, for instance, in cleanin' up on this affectionate uncle of yours, why—you can count on James Bryce."

"You're very kind." The girl's eyes were wide and dark. "I don't know right now how to thank you."

"You don't need to," Jim told her sincerely. "I guess I'd get thanks enough in just the job itself. Such things make me sick." And he really looked it, as he sat there scowling, his brows drawn together, his stubby brown mustache pursed out over his lip.

Here, then, I thought was another surface stirring in the course of the whole affair, a quivering of the surface that once more hinted of some greater disturbance, some deeper, darker, more sinister element, moving unseen in the depths, another incident in what I had come to call the invisible course of the matter, not in its way unlike the triangular dorsal fin of a shark, cutting the sun-lighted wave to mark the course of the destroying monster underneath.

"Come, dear." Marya Harding was speaking; she drew the girl to her feet.

Bryce and I rose. The episode was ended in so far as I could see. The girl was free, and as Marya had assured her, safe, I fancied. Her escape had been well-nigh soundless. They would hardly think of looking for her here in this fashionable house. Here she could lie hid, and recuperate, until she was ready, in a time—probably, as I thought now, of Dual's selection—to step forth, to confront, confound, and condemn those by whom she had been so greatly wronged. Gripping as it was in itself, it was no more than an episode, indeed.

"Then, we'll say good night—or good morning," I suggested. "How do we go out?"

She went quickly toward the front door. Jim and I trailed behind her. But just inside the door I paused.

"She'll need medical attention, won't she?" I questioned. "And, under the circumstances, will it, or won't it, be difficult?"

"Under the circumstances it will not." Marya's dark eyes shot a twinkling glance into my face. "I have a harmless sleeping powder for her tonight, and in the morning Dr. Simpson will see her and take charge."

She drew the door open. We passed outside, and went down the walk to the street before either of us spoke. And then, as usual, it was Bryce who broke forth once more in a heavy rumble of half-comprehension, half-bewilderment:

"Simpson. Well, I am damned. So that's why Semi wanted to meet him. It beats me. On the level it beats me, Glace."

I nodded. Dual had said everything would be explained, or explain itself, and seemingly once more his promise was verified.

"It beats both of us, Jim, and I think it's calculated to beat this whole infernal proposition," I agreed.

CHAPTER XVI

BREAKING UP THE HOUSE

YET, EVEN SO, the course of the thing was to be marked by other surface stirrings, other incidents, and other episodes.

Two days after the night when Gladys Ashton was released from the House of Invisible Bondage, John Parkins, president of the Parkins-Mahlberg Trust Company, took a gun from the drawer of a deck in his ovate office, and shot himself.

Once more the headlines flared. The thing was suicide beyond any doubt. The man had left the usual letters. But, to Bryce and me, his act was more than it appeared to the man in the street. Practically a bankrupt, he had ended a losing struggle. But over and above that, his death was a confirmation of Gladys Ashton's story to both of us.

As Jim summed it up. "If that girl's dippy, I'm a babbling idiot. She never was adjudged insane, I guess. Parkins just paid Drake to hold her while he looted her estate. Your affectionate uncle, John Parkins, deceased. Say, if Johnson knew the insides of this he'd have the pip."

But Johnson didn't know, or the police. Parkins' financial breakdown seemed motive enough for his act. I found myself marveling more and more at this further illustration of how little the world really knew of what went on, back and behind the scenes.

And the next day Jim came in again with a paper, and a heavy finger marking a personal advertisement. "Read that," he said:

Information is desired leading to a meeting with Miss Gladys

Ashton, sole heir and executrix under the will of John Parkins, of the Parkins-Mahlberg Trust Company, deceased. Good and Dunn, Attorneys, Stroller Building.

I read it, and looked into my partner's eyes. They were narrowed. "Peachy. Sort of cute, ain't it?" he said. "Gladys hopped hit, as Kingsley might remark. By the way, that bird seems to be about himself, Johnson says. But comin' back to our pork chops, Gladys has melted into thin air, an' they darsent raise a fuss, especially now that old John has gracefully shuffled off. So they advertise, an' bait the hook. Just the same, I wonder how much Drake had to do with Parkins' death."

"Blackmail?" I suggested.

"Beaucoup pennies probably," he replied. "Why not? After John had got 'm to hold the girl, why, naturally, they had him in a trap. He couldn't let her go, and he couldn't refuse to cough up. It's peachy, as I said."

"It's damnable," I growled. "But, about this advertisement. What can they expect to gain by getting hold of her now?"

"Gain?" Jim grinned. "Why, buy her off, get her to sell 'em immunity for some of her own pennies back on a bet. That little lady can raise Billy Hades with Drake if she likes when she comes out of Marya's house, where she's layin' doggo right now. That is, she can if she likes."

He was right, too. But I wondered, none the less. Beyond discovering through Johnson, again, that Kingsley was to be kept at the county hospital for a time, and Dual's message, sending us to meet Marya, we had heard nothing from Semi since. Yet, here was something I felt he ought to know.

"You may be right," I rejoined. "But suppose we go up, and show this thing to Dual, and see what he says."

What Semi actually said, however, had more to do with Parkins' death than the personal advertisement.

He read the latter, and tossed the paper aside. "Have I not said that selfishness, treachery, false dealing, and the like were unstable foundations on which to rear a life's superstructure?"

he observed. "And is it not proved in this suicide of a man who was guilty of their employment in his treatment of his sister's child? Have the soul sands on which he sought to build to his own advantage not opened and dragged him down at the last? Only those things endure which are builded on righteousness."

"But this ad?" Bryce prompted. "Do you think it genuine, or a trap?"

Semi Dual eyed him. "Let be, let be," he replied at length. "Let time answer it. Is the maid not safe? Is she not recovering health, and strength?"

"Under Simpson?" Jim suggested.

"Under Simpson's care." Semi's gray eyes twinkled, I thought.

"And this place of Drake's?" Bryce turned his question to another point.

"A House of Invisible Bondage, as I have called it. Another house builded upon the sand," said Semi Dual. "It, too, shall fall as a house of cards."

Jim nodded. "Well, that's good. Justice seems to have been done in the case of Parkins, at all events."

"And the law will take its course against any man who runs counter to it," Dual returned.

"Bo-Peep's comin' home, Marya Harding says," Jim continued. "You know it?"

Semi inclined his head.

"But Imer hasn't been turned loose."

"Nay, but he will be before long, I think."

Once more Jim grinned. "Is there anything you'd like to say this mornin' before we leave?" he inquired with good-natured impudence.

And Semi Dual's lips twitched slightly. "What is to be will be, my friend."

"Oh, yes," said Jim, and stood up. "The clock, eh—this here, now, astrological alarm clock again. Did you and Simpson decide that Kingsley was a nut, or just a brainstorm case, or what?"

"We concurred in Dr. Drake's estimation of the matter that the man Kingsley would very shortly be himself again," Semi returned.

Jim gave it up, but he chuckled once we had left the tower. "Just the same, he knows what's what," he declared. "He's dead sure of it by this time, son. He never talks quite like that unless he does. He's got that web of his all woven, an' he's dead certain it's strong enough to hold."

I nodded. "I think so, Jim," I assented.

"He knows. He knows," Jim repeated, and puffed furiously at his cigar. "By golly, son, it's rich. I bet that there House of Invisible Bondage is more like a beehive these last few days. Gladys beats it, and Parkins pulls a suicide.

"Drake must be just about matchin' pennies to see where he gets off. An' whisper this to the pines, my boy—he ain't goin' to get off, whether he knows it or not. Not if that net of Semi's holds. As a straw gatherer my hat's off to Henri. That baby certainly is good."

"Gladys's bustin' out should prove a pretty heavy straw, too. An' you can see how Semi's goin' to use her; just keep her under cover till he's ready; then bingo! She won't be just a straw; she'll be more like a whole stack."

"Possibly that's what Parkins thought," I suggested.

We were still talking it over as we entered the office, and found Johnson seated in my private room with his hat on top of my desk.

"Hello," he greeted. "Say, there's an ad in the paper about a niece of Parkins, this mornin'. Seen it, have you, Bryce?"

"Oh, yes. He's seen it. I see you know he's a newspaper addict," I returned before Jim had more than nodded.

"I was up to see Good an' Dunn about it," Johnson resumed. "There's something funny the way Parkins seems to have took his high dive. Their ad's straight. Parkins left a will naming her heir an' executrix, if alive."

"If alive?" I repeated. "Didn't he know whether she was or not?"

"That's the question," Johnson declared. "He ought to, because—here's the funny stuff—he kept her the last year over here in Doc Drake's place. Not crazy, you understand, just troubled with her nerves. Seems he'd mentioned it to Good before, asked him to look after the girl in case anything ever happened to him, and then he makes this will an' mails it to him, the day he killed himself.

"So Good calls up this joint of Drake's, an' finds out the girl had disappeared, run off two nights before the suicide; an' Drake swears he don't know where she is. So Good runs the ad."

"Yeah?" Jim walked over and stood looking out of a window. I fancied he didn't care to look Johnson in the face. It was plain enough he knew nothing beyond the facts he had mentioned, and Jim manifestly felt he might read our greater knowledge in his expression.

"Yeah. Furthermore," Johnson ran on, "along with the will was a letter of instructions to Good and Dunn, and another letter addressed to this Gladys Ashton—that was the girl's name—to be delivered only to her, or in the event of her failing to appear within a year, to be destroyed unopened."

"Which means that Parkins knew she had disappeared before he shot himself," I said.

"Seemingly," Johnson assented quickly. "That's the point."

"If you'll look it up," I told him, "you'll find that Gladys Ashton's mother left a large fortune when she died, and left it not in part to her brother, but wholly to her child. Gladys broke down after her mother's death, and Parkins seems to have taken care of her since."

"Taken care of her is right." Jim spoke without turning around.

"Well, by the Lord!" Johnson exclaimed. "Parkins, was a plunger, I know, but holy smoke! Good and Dunn asked the office to try an' help find this girl, last night. That's how I got into it. What do you know about it—anything else?"

"A lot more than you do," Jim spun around. "An' what we don't, we can guess. Let it alone. Stall these lawyers off. If you don't, you're apt to tip over the beans. Johnson—" he came across and stared full into his old pal's eyes—"what would you say if I was to tell you that girl is right here in this city?"

"I'd say you knew where she was!" Johnson narrowed his lids.

And Bryce nodded. He knew his man, knew he was deserving of trust, a man who had devoted the best of his life to the interests of law, and order, and justice. "Yes, an' you'd be right," he averred. "And what would you say if I was to tell you further that Doc Simpson is takin' care of her right now, tryin' to undo Drake's work?"

"I'd say Semi Dual," Johnson told him. I saw comprehension flash in his eyes. "So that's it, eh? Let's see; that bird said justice was goin' to be done, an' the law take its course. He's gunnin' for Drake."

"He's gunnin' for anybody that needs gunnin' for," Jim returned with emphasis. "An' he's goin' to get 'em, Johnson. He put Simpson on this girl's case. He's watchin' 'em, Johnson, watchin' 'em like a hawk, beatin' 'em to it, copperin' their every bet, their every move. Hold up your tryin' to find this girl until he's ready to use her. Don't go to mussin' into it now."

He stood facing the inspector; the two men looked deep into one another's eyes. And then Johnson nodded slowly in the way of one who reaches a decision. "All right, Jimmie," he yielded. "Keep your shirt on. I'll lay off. But ask him to let me find her when he's ready."

"You're on, if it's possible, Johnnie." Jim stuck out his hand.

And Johnson shook hands with him.

"All right then, Jim, that's tended to," he said. "I'll be gettin' along. Drake was just sort of keepin' her for Parkins at that rate."

Bryce nodded. "Yes, the dirty crook."

"Considerin' which he ought to be about as nervous as a fish," our visitor suggested.

"Yeah." Suddenly Bryce grinned. "And whether he is or not, from now on, he's apt to get about as far as a hen on a settin' of addled eggs—"

"Which ain't far," Johnson decided. "Well—so long. Slip me the office any time you're needin' help."

"The greatest help you can give us right now is to do nothin'," Bryce told him.

He mumbled farewell, and stalked out.

But despite his prognostication that Drake might be somewhat disturbed by the course of recent events, another two days passed without any happening of apparent interest to us.

Then, however, Imer Lamb was released. As was to be expected, the daily press bulletined the fact. Not only that, but two other inmates of the House of Bondage were taken with Lamb before a commission, and adjudged sane as a preliminary to their release. As Jim expressed it, Drake appeared to have organized a "graduating class."

"Four in the last few days. One lost, an' three turned out. Well, anyway, he's goin' to save somethin' on board bills," he observed.

Lamb, however, having in his return to liberty verified Semi Dual's prediction that such a return would occur, proceeded to plunge himself into the limelight of public interest at once.

The night after his release he entertained a party on the Glen Arms roof. The thing was duly noted in the next morning papers. The subsequent afternoon, he motored to the aviation field, and took up his plane for an exhibition of flying such as had not been seen in local aviation circles for many years.

If there was a bit of trick work, a breathtaking stunt of aerial evolution which he did not perform, to judge from the next day's story, his omission of it from his program was a matter of oversight merely, and not intent. His plane had seemingly never been on a level keel for more than a few minutes at a stretch. It dived and climbed, turned, and twisted, and looped. It seemed to have literally writhed in the air in a series of gymnastics through which it was difficult to imagine that its glistening fabric could have lived.

"The Mad Aviator" some unthinking reporter called him in an enthusiasm born of his amazing antics, perhaps. One didn't like to think it was more than unthinkingness. The mad aviator—and Imer Lamb but just released, from an institution designed for the treatment of mental conditions. Not but what he did in the air would have seemed to justify the title, but because the name stuck. And because Lamb kept it up.

He continued to act in a fashion calculated to deserve his name. His flying became a sensation, a dread, an ordeal at the flying field. Out there no one doubted but sooner or later he would crash his plane; the thing was inevitable in the opinion of all the field attendants. Indirectly I heard that they had deliberately formed a pool, based on their expectations of the event.

It drew an audience. More and more those seeking a morbid thrill drove out to park their cars, and watch that solo aerial circus which could some day have but one horribly certain end; for Imer Lamb now did only solo flying. Where formerly he had frequently taken up a mechanic with him, he now consistently left the man behind. There was a sinister import in the action that hinted at only one thing.

"Tryin' to kill himself," Bryce growled his comment. "Tryin' to break his neck an' make it look like an accident. Anybody can see it. Maybe he ain't crazy, but his flyin' is pure insane."

I nodded. I had long before reached the same conclusion in my own mind.

It was not a pleasant thought, hinting as it did of what the man's own thoughts must be. But it was the only plausible explanation of his actions one could entertain. I thought of Bo-Peep, the little Venus Semi had urged away.

In a way I think I prayed for her return. If she came back— if she wept to him or called him to her—she might be able to stop this mad courting of death on which he had engaged. I even found myself wondering if her absence could be one of the causes back of the thing.

Yet if so, if it were in any sense a major cause, it seemed odd to me that Dual should have let her Western visit drag so long. It was not like him. His study of their conjoined charts must have shown him the danger. And such a danger he would not, I felt sure, have ignored.

Yet, meanwhile, Imer laughed ribaldry into the faces of those who sought to stay him, and became a veritable demon of the air, who balked not at anything. Careless of all consequences, he yet seemed possessed of a charmed life that defied all mischance in any spectacular evolution he undertook, and brought him back again and again to the ground with a half-contemptuous smile for the strained eyes of those who had watched him.

Then one day Jim entered my room for the third time with an afternoon paper, and plunked himself into a chair.

"Well," he remarked, "I'm gettin' to be a regular society news hound, an' I see Bo-Peep's got home. Now maybe she'll take a hand in this game, and snap a leading string on her Lamb."

But the next morning, Dual called us to the roof, and we answered the summons, and found Moira Mason, herself, strained of face, as one is strained in the grip of some numbing emotion, seated with him in the inner tower room.

CHAPTER XVII

THE CONFERENCE
IN THE TOWER

MOIRA MASON WAS white. All color seemed drained from her. Shadows lay under her blue eyes. Her appearance shocked me. One felt that the faith and hope she had said so confidently should support her had deserted her instead.

The last time I had seen her Bo-Peep had been so much more her normal self, even if a bit disturbed, a bit uncertain. Lamb and his mad course since his release had rendered her haggard with fright.

Bryce though was more natural, less formal than myself in his surprise.

"Bo-Peep—what the devil's happened now?" he exclaimed.

"Wait," Semi Dual spoke, before she could possibly answer. "Much has happened—and most of it of import to us who would undo a wrong, and make straight a crooked path. That you may hear of it I have called here this morning in order that, having heard it, you may once more render aid. Some little Miss Mason has told me. Yet she shall tell it again, and perchance at greater length. Be seated."

Jim and I found chairs.

"And now, Moira," Semi prompted. "Speak to us those things within thy heart, and speak as one speaks to friends."

"I didn't know. I hadn't heard a whisper of it till I got home," Bo-Peep began. "Imer's dreadful flying I mean. I didn't even know he had been released until after I had reached my home, and called his brother on the phone. Then he told me, and said he must see me at once. It surprised me greatly. He'd never been very friendly.

"But he was so urgent that I said he might come. And then I called Imer's apartments, and a strange man answered and said he was Imer's valet, but that he wasn't there at present, but out at the flying field. I was surprised when he said he was Imer's man, because he'd had Joe Kingsley for years, and I didn't know about Joe either until after I saw George.

"I left word for Imer to call my number, and then George came and told me about Imer's flying. I'd never seen him quite as he was. He was frightened. I could see he was frightened, and he asked me, told me I must make Imer stop, because if he kept on he was practically certain to be killed. I asked him what made him do such a thing, and he hesitated a minute and then said he didn't know.

"But some way I knew that he lied. Then he went on and told me about Joe after I had asked him why Imer had a new man. And after I'd promised to do what I could with Imer he left; and I waited until I couldn't stand it, and then took my car and drove out to the field. Imer had just come down. I stopped as near to his hangar as I could, and when he came out and walked toward his own motor I called his name.

"He was laughing, and even after he saw me he kept right on laughing. But he came over. 'Hello, Moira,' he said. 'Wasn't expecting you back.' He was very casual about it, almost as though I hadn't been out of town.

" 'Imer,' I said, and looked straight in his eyes. 'Imer, what is the meaning of this?'

"And he set his lips, and looked very strange—almost as though I had some way hurt him. 'Rather hard to answer that here, dear girl,' he said. 'But I'll see you this evening, if I may, and explain.'

"I asked him if I couldn't drive him back, and he set his jaws again, almost as though he were gritting his teeth, and refused.

And I drove home alone. I was dreadfully worried. You see, I couldn't understand, not then.

"But he came to me that evening just as he had promised, and then I did understand what they'd done to him in that dreadful place—how they'd ruined his life and mine. He was hurt by finding I'd gone away before he got out too.

"And I couldn't tell him, before I'd seen you, Mr. Dual. But I did tell him there was a reason—a very good reason—which, when I could tell him, he would understand. And when I said that he laughed again, and said it didn't matter.

" 'Why, Imer—why?' I asked.

"And then he told me. You see he doesn't think he is still quite sane. He doesn't think he is insane at present, but that dreadful man, Dr. Drake, told him, before he was turned loose, that while he was all right now, and in his estimation would remain so; still the history of cases which had once exhibited symptoms of a homicidal nature was that they might at any time recur."

"The infernal hound!" Jim's ejaculation cut into the sound of her voice.

In a flash I saw what Drake, for some purpose of his own, had done—how he had turned Imer Lamb out of his institution with a suggestion of a recurrence of his recent affliction to ride him haggle the rest of his life.

It was an infernal, a fiendish thing. It was diabolical. My mind balked at a term foul enough to describe the thing. And it had

been cold-blooded, deliberate I thought of Drake's first assurance to me that Lamb would soon return to a practical normal,
and I began to understand. It had been part of a thought-out
scheme.

I saw Moira Mason's eyes turn to Jim to Semi, to me, and
back to Dual again. "You see what he had done," she resumed.
"He had set him free, but with that terrible thought in his brain.
I cried out that I didn't believe it. But it made no impression on
him. He said that the mere chance that it was true spelled the
end of all things between us—that he would never marry, never
consider marriage as long as he felt that he carried an unsound
spot in his brain.

"And when he said that I—I—" for the first time a faint tinge
of color crept into her white cheeks…" I threw myself into his
arms, told him I was sure it was all false that—that I was willing
to prove my faith by marrying him at once.

"But it wasn't any use. He held me, he was very gentle; but
he was so dreadfully, terribly strong. He was strong enough to
refuse me. He stood firm in his determination—he held me,
talked to me, and then at the end—he kissed me. It wasn't just
good night—it was good-by."

"And he's flying again this afternoon. He told me he would
before he kissed me good-by and went. And I can't stand it—I
can't stand it!"

She clenched her hands. "I can't let him. It means just one
thing. He won't come back; he doesn't mean to come back if
he flies this afternoon. I don't know. If I'd never gone away—
perhaps. But now—now—"

"Peace, child." Dual's mellow voice struck bell-like into the
gasping phrases of her emotion. "Had you not gone, could you
then have rendered your fullest help to him?"

Her eyes turned toward him. They were wide, dark. I watched
her, this girl who was fighting so hard for her mate. And, too,
I saw now the measure of that man; Imer Lamb had become a
figure to excite my admiration as one who did what he thought

right, refused to pander to self no matter what it might mean to him. It had been a final farewell his lips had conveyed to Moira's lips. This afternoon he would no longer leave his fate to chance. He would seek, and find it in a quick and whirling plunge.

Her pale lips moved. "No, of course not," they whispered. "If I had not gone, done what you told me, I could not have brought back proof of those things you felt must be proved. But—to come back with it, feeling I was bringing help to him, and then to have what is happening this afternoon happen—to find they had wrecked all the future while I was gone."

"Wrecked?" Dual's tone expressed a question that seemed to catch her up, to excite other thoughts in her brain.

"Oh, I've tried to be strong," she cried. "I've tried to have faith, hope, to go on. I've done everything I could, everything you said, as nearly as I could. I've brought back proof of everything you said I must."

"Everything?" Dual questioned again

"I think so," she returned. "I found why Drake left Los Angeles, where he practiced. I found out that Nathalie Norton is not Nathalie Norton really, but his sister."

"What's that?" Jim rose half out of his chair.

Nathalie Norton, George Lamb's intimate friend, was Nathalie Drake, the sister of the man who had been so greatly involved in the affairs of Imer Lamb.

"Yes." I heard Moira speaking. "She was in pictures, as you know, for a time till Drake had to leave California. Then she came here with him, and met George Lamb.

"I think George is scared, dreadful frightened, since he sees that this affair is going to result in Imer's death. He was frightened yesterday afternoon. But he lied; I knew he lied when he said he didn't know. There was a guilty knowledge in his eyes. I—oh—why can't men learn that women feel such things? He knows—I sure of it."

"He knows," said Semi Dual. "Listen Venus, did I not say in the beginning that you should greatly aid—and have you not done so since that time? Yet listen further, and possess thyself in peace. Let not the clouds of doubt and lack of understanding affright you as a child is affrighted in the night by an ugly dream.

"He knows—and Uranus is a sign of explosive nature. Uranus is sometime named in astrology as the policeman of the Sun. Uranus in the present instance is drawing ever closer to that overlord of his, to the time when Neptune and Mars shall feel the flaming fury of the Sun himself and thereby be destroyed.

"Child, think you that I have sat idle while you have worked? Did I not say to you that Jupiter was the judge? Nay, I worked and watched, and marked every move in this sorry matter. Even in the matter of thy lover's flying I have not intervened. For a man dies at the time when his death is written, and my study of the life chart of Imer Lamb has shown me that his death is not to come upon him for years—many years."

"You mean—oh—do you mean that?" Bo-Peep cried out, while again I saw the explanation of Semi's seemingly paradoxical actions at which I had marveled and now marveled once again.

He answered her softly: "Know you who the man was who answered you yesterday afternoon from the rooms of Imer Lamb?"

"No."

"Henri," said Semi Dual. "My own man—the man I sent into this unclean house of Hugo Drake's to watch over thy beloved and at the same time to learn many things."

"Henri—your own man?" Moira asked.

"Henri," Dual repeated, "who won thy lover's liking and confidence, who went with him by my orders to watch over him still, after his own man, the British ex-soldier, Joseph Kingsley, fell an unintended victim to the working out of others' plans. Peace, child. While you have worked under my direction, and seen my assumptions proved in a concrete fashion thus far, I have watched. Thy lover will not fly this afternoon."

"Will not?" she questioned, and lifted a hand to her throat, where the words were half strangled.

"Nay. Have I not called my friends, those whom I named my satellites, to me? Are they not present to take my commands? That which is to be will be, Moira—but not before its time. Hence, listen again and attend to my words, as to how this thing shall be done."

For a moment he paused, and his glance swept from her to me, to Bryce, before he resumed.

"Henri, my friend and companion, has watched and reported everything. Ye, my friends, shall now intervene. You will go to the rooms of Imer Lamb this afternoon at half after one.

"But you shall not go before, since before you go Henri shall have been withdrawn with no word of explanation to the man to whom he has rendered attendance. This shall perhaps impress that man as strange. But you shall go to him, and say that you know that his man has gone. And you shall say to him that he was but the trusted agent of one who has watched the progress of this whole matter from the first because the woman who loves him, the woman he loves, requested him to do so.

"And you shall invite him into the presence of this unknown friend of them, both the friend of his mate to be, the friend of his vanished man. You shall ask him to come with you. He has seen you. He may even vaguely remember the time—after his arrest and incarceration at the jail—when you called upon him. Remind him of it, if the need arise.

"And say further that shall he accompany you here to my quarters he will get an explanation of this matter which shall make all plain and convince him that there is not, never has been, any real or material derangement of his reason, since all that has happened is but the working out of a corrupt scheme.

"Drowning men grasp at straws, my friends. I do not think Imer Lamb will refuse you after you have spoken to him thus and he has a glimpse of the future and all it may hold for him."

"Oh—oh—" Moira Mason was sobbing.

But, to me, there was a hint of relaxing tension in the sound.

"And thou, Venus," Dual addressed her as I glanced at Bryce and saw comprehension and eager understanding in his eyes, "who have aided greatly, you shall aid yet more in one thing. Return from me here to thy own home and make use of the telephone.

"Upon it call the office of George Lamb, or seek him elsewhere until found. Say to him then that last night you failed to redeem the promise made to him as regards his brother; that he refused you, broke your engagement, bade you farewell, and announced his intention of flying this afternoon. Make plain to him that his decision appeared unalterable to you at that time."

"And then?" Moira questioned, her expression mystified and startled.

"Nay," said Semi Dual. "Have you yet found me lacking of a reason for those things I directed in anything?"

"Oh, no," she answered quickly. "Forgive me. I've been so terribly frightened. But I might have known. I think maybe I did know in my soul—even if I couldn't see any way out in my brain. At least I brought all my trouble to you again. And I'll go now."

"Aye, go," Dual assented, rising. "I have much to which I must attend. But the time is short until that time when everything, even to the smallest detail of this matter, shall be plain. Go, then, Moira—Venus—and ye, too, my friends."

The three of us left the tower and passed down through the garden toward the stairs.

"Oh," she half spoke, half sobbed, "I feel so sorry, so ashamed. I've disappointed him so. I've been so weak at the end."

"An' don't you doubt for a minute but he understands it, Bo-Peep," Jim told her. "Semi Dual don't only read minds and stars; he reads the hearts of his fellowmen. My great aunt, Miss Mason, what you've gone through is enough to break any girl's nerve! You've been amazing, immense.

"An' don't you see what he's doing to George by having you call him and tell him you failed last night? Didn't he say Uranus is explosive—an' ain't George Uranus, just as you are Venus an' Gordon an' me are satellites?

"An' explosive things have a habit of blowin' up. Oh, Pip! It's a dead open an' shut proposition—dead open an' shut. When you slip that to Lamb, an' he feels sure Imer's goin' out to commit suicide this afternoon, he's goin' to simply blow up with a loud noise.

"I'd sure like to hear it, but I won't. I'll be over with Gordon, persuadin' that boy of yours that his brain ain't as moth-eaten as Doc Drake said it was."

"You really think so?" Moira Mason questioned. Renewed hope and a reborn faith were in her eyes.

"Do I?" Jim grinned. "Well, I'd bet a million on it; an' since I ain't got it, I'd be a total ruin if I lost."

And suddenly, unexpectedly, Moira Mason laughed—though her laughter still held the sound of unshed tears.

On the seventh floor we left her and walked toward the office. "George is Uranus—an' Nathalie Norton is Drake's sister," Jim growled. "Can you beat it, son, can you beat it? No answer. You can't. But I suspected George was Uranus all along, remember. An' he is. Uranus, the policeman of the Sun. Do you get it? Moira is goin' to blow him up when she gets him, an' he's goin' to spill. At that rate Uranus is just about goin' to arrest himself. Dual sure is the serpent's hips. I—"

He threw open the door of the outer office and paused.

Norman Haddon sat there, cool, immaculate in dress, smiling as our glances met. Norman Haddon, Federal secret agent, a man we had known, worked with more than once in past years, dark, debonair, more like a society dilettante in speech and bearing than a man of keenly analytical mind and inflexible nerve.

"Haddon—what the deuce are you doing here?" I exclaimed, as Jim emitted a sort of inarticulate grunt of both recognition and surprise.

CHAPTER XVIII

A FRIEND DROPS IN

"**WAITIN' FOR YOU** chaps, old top," Norman Haddon returned as he rose and took my hand. "Just waitin' to say 'bon jour' or 'buenos dias,' as you prefer, I'm a bird of passage, you know. Flit here, flit there, never long in one place. In town for a day or two. Thought I'd look you up. Old friends, you know, and all that sort of rot. Also Dual, wonderful chap. Expect to see him too before I flit somewhere else."

"Well, suppose you flit into my private room over here first," I suggested, smiling in spite of myself at his affected speech, which was as much of a mask as anything else, as I had long ago found out.

"Righto!" he accepted, and accompanied Jim and me inside the room, the door of which I closed. I turned as Haddon sat down. "Now talk English. Is this just a friendly call, or isn't it?"

"Oh, but—" His eyes twinkled. "On the level, Glace, you're a suspicious chap. Can't even a J.D. man make a call on a friend or two without standing a third degree from a private 'tec?"

"He can," I said, grinning. "And the friend will be decidedly glad to see him. Where've you been since our last meeting down on the Mexican border?"

"Here and there," he explained without apparently any considerable interest. "Los Angeles last. And that reminds me, I met an acquaintance of yours in the Angel City. A Miss Moira Mason, charming little lady."

"Bo-Peep?" At last Bryce found his voice in a rasping fashion.

"Eh?" Haddon eyed him. "Well, really, I can't say, old dear. Are you one of her sheep? As I recall, the lady lost them, and there was no mention of goats. I raise the point merely because my idea of a sheep hardly fits the picture. But a goat now—that bit of cabbage in your mouth—"

Jim grinned, and removed his cigar from between his teeth. "Some time ago a lamb took exceptions to my particular brand of tobacco," he growled.

"And the lamb?" Haddon suggested.

"Was adjudged insane," Jim told him.

"Moira's, not Mary's, Lamb, eh?" Suddenly knowledge leaped at both of us in Haddon's words.

Haddon knew; then his call was not a casual visit.

"By th' Lord!" Jim fairly howled. "Haddon, kick in! Come through! She was down there—met you? Did Dual have you meet her?"

"Well, he did suggest it." Haddon smiled.

"And what did you find out? What did you two do?"

"Oh, we looked up an address." Haddon shrugged. "That is, I did after she had furnished the address."

"And you found?" Bryce was leaning forward.

"Enough." Again Haddon shrugged. And then he sobered, his provocative manner dropped from him, sloughed off. "Enough, Bryce," he said. "Quite enough to make a lot of trouble for the man who lived there. He doesn't live there now. But—that's all for the present. I wired Dual I was coming, and I have an appointment with him for eleven."

He glanced at his watch. "We'll have to go into it later. As a matter of fact, though, there is quite a tale behind Moira's Lamb, as I suspect. You probably know that as well as I do. She told me you we interested in the case. See you some more." He stood up.

"Haddon!" Bryce fairly mouthed after the Government agent had taken himself off. "Moira met him—" he made a pin down there by Semi's direction—"now what the devil!"

"Jim," I said. All at once I saw it or thought I did. "Jim, do you remember what Dual just told us to tell Imer this afternoon—that there is not, never has been, any actual trouble with his reason. Material trouble, he said. That means any actual trouble with his brain. See here, has it ever occurred to you that Imer Lamb may have been driven insane by drugs?"

"Drugs?" he parroted, but I saw the stirrings of comprehension in his eyes.

"Yes, something has made him temporarily insane—something has gradually upset his mental balance, something that having once produced the effect could be gradually withdrawn?"

"Good Lord!" he scowled. "I know Haddon's done a lot of work in the narcotic division of the department, but—how was it worked?"

"Use your head," I told him. "Imer Lamb had one excessive habit—smoking."

"Gordon!" He sprang up. And now I saw he understood. "That's it. They mixed it with his tobacco. He smoked special brand, he and George both; Kingsley said so."

"Yes, and Kingsley said he scragged, as he expressed it, a pipeful now and then, if you'll remember," I returned, "And when Lamb was taken to jail he must have left some of it in his rooms. We know he did because according to Kingsley again, Drake went there to get it the day Kingsley attacked him, and—"

"Yes, an' Kingsley had been smoking it after Imer left," Jim broke in. "That's it, son' He smoked it right along while he was alone, an' it got in its work on him. You know Dual said his blow-off was an unexpected thing in the working out of others' plans.

"It works out. It's riveted. That's why Drake went after the stuff; that's why he was so damned sure Imer would recover. They took him over there, an' took him off the stuff, whatever it was, an' they didn't want that old supply he'd left to be in his dump when he went back there again!"

"You've got it, Jim," I agreed. At last the thing was plain. As he said, it was right. It matched up. Here, then, in our deductions, once more Dual's assertion that Imer Lamb was mentally sound was verified. We could go to him this afternoon and deliver that message to his troubled soul in absolute confidence, a confidence that could scarcely fail to carry conviction to his only too willing mind.

We took a taxi. It put us down at Monk's Hall, at half past one o'clock. Ignoring the desk, we took the elevator to Lamb's floor, and went directly to his suite and rang.

Imer Lamb opened the door himself. I noted the fact with satisfaction. Henri was gone then; everything was working out.

"Good afternoon, Mr. Lamb. May we come in?" I said.

He regarded us with a slightly questioning frown. "Would you employ force if I refused?" he suggested.

"Why, no," I said. "But we might use argument. Have you forgotten us, Mr. Lamb—Mr. Glace, and my partner, Mr. Bryce?"

"Glace and Bryce." His frown deepened in an effort at association. "Frankly, Mr. Glace, I seem to have seen you somewhere, but I've no clear recollection. You'll pardon it, I trust. Come in."

We entered the suite, and he gave us chairs. "You saw us at the jail after they took you there, and I gave you a cigar, and you said it was a filthy bit of tobacco," Bryce remarked with his at times bludgeon-like directness as we sat down.

"I did?" Lamb said quickly. "Okay but—you see, at that time I was scarcely myself, as I hope you understand. I'm sorry."

"That was said merely to recall the incident, Mr. Lamb," I told him, watching his face. It was haggard, worn, its eyes hot and feverish as they turned to me from Jim. "Our errand here this afternoon is to bear you an invitation from a friend. You see, we are acquainted with your man Henri, who has been your personal companion and attendant for some time, but who left you this morning."

"Henri?" His expression showed a sudden quickened interest. "You know that, do you? Well, if you do, possibly you can tell me where he's gone. As you say, he left me today, and without a word of warning. He was here this morning when I went out for a time, and gone when I returned. I found it a bit odd. He'd been an ideal fellow, and I'd come to depend on him. Had intelligence; used his brain—"

"All of that, Mr. Lamb," I interrupted. "But what would you say if I were to tell you, as I am here to tell you, that he was merely lent to you as an attendant first at Dr. Drake's institution, and later here by this other friend of yours from whom we come?"

"A friend?" he said. "Really, Mr. Glace, I'm afraid I don't understand. You say he lent him to me?"

"Following a suggestion made by Miss Moira Mason, the young lady to whom at the time of your present trouble you were engaged. She—"

"Just a moment," he checked me sharply. "I'm not discussing personal matters, you'll please understand, Mr. Glace."

"After she had gone to this friend whose companion Henri was," I ignored his interruption, "first coming to us with Mrs. Marya Harding—"

"Wait. I know Mrs. Harding, certainly," he again interposed. "You say Moira—"

"Came to us with her in order that she might meet this other friend, who lent Henri to her as your attendant, and ask his aid."

"What are you trying to tell me?" he demanded as I paused.

"I'm trying to tell you that through all your trouble you have had an unknown friend, Mr. Lamb," I replied.

"An unknown friend?" Again he knit his brows.

"Who says there ain't anything wrong with your head, an' never was, an' never will be so far as he knows." Bryce suddenly threw his amazing statement at him.

For a long time Imer Lamb said nothing. And then he drew a deep and slightly audible breath. His lips set, the spandrels of his nostrils flared. His eyes turned from me to Jim. They seemed to probe, plumb, search.

"Who says, in other words, that I am sane?"

"Absolutely." Bryce nodded.

And again there was silence, while Imer Lamb wrestled with that positive declaration, seemed to strive to match it up with all that had been, all that had occurred, all that to him was now a past knowledge which, were Jim's words true, became something less than fact.

"Then, just what was the matter with me?" he finally asked, his lip curling a trifle in a way to indicate unbelief.

And, because it seemed best to me to do so, I left it to Bryce to answer: "You was doped."

"I was what?" Lamb's expression altered again.

"Drugged," Jim told him. "At least that's what we suspect—just as we suspect they had it in that tobacco you smoked so much before you went off your nut."

"Good Lord!" Lamb brought the words out in a hoarse gasp. Consternation, and a dawning comprehension were in his face. He seemed dazed. Belief, at least what I thought might be a wish to believe, struggled with unbelief within him in so far as I could judge. He left his chair and walked the length of the room, pausing beside the table whereon was the tobacco jar I had seen the day I came there with Jim, after Kingsley had attacked Drake, the jar that had seemed so innocent a thing then, and yet might well have held the very agency of its owner's undoing if what seemed so probable now were right.

For a time, difficult to measure mentally, he stood looking down upon it. One could imagine him seeking to give it full value, questioning, arguing with himself, seeking to determine all it had meant, all it might mean yet to him in view of what he had heard. Presently he turned and came back.

"But I got my tobacco from my brother. He smoked the same brand after he discovered it. It was a blend he got from a friend. I always obtained it from him."

"Well?" Bryce dragged his comment across his tongue.

The eyes of the two men met.

They met, and held through an interval of silence.

Then: "There is a rather unpleasant implication in that, don't you think, Mr. Bryce," Imer Lamb said. "Hadn't you better explain?"

"As a matter of fact, Mr. Lamb," I again took part before Jim had seemingly decided upon an answer, "we would hardly be here—hardly venture even indirectly to suggest such a possibility, as I see you recognize, unless in our estimation it were fully possible of being supported by proof."

"That my brother George was a party, to—to what was done?" he queried, once more frowning as though he found the thought hard to accept.

"We have every reason at least to think so," I reaffirmed. "As I told you, practically every step in this whole affair has been watched by the man from whom we come. In that watching we have had some little part. We are not making any accusation blindly."

"But for Heaven's sake, Mr. Glace," he exclaimed, "you're asking me to believe that I've been the victim of a cowardly bit of work—that I've been tricked, deceived in every way, duped. And if you're right—" He paused and once more drew a deep and slightly unsteady breath. An expression of swift appreciation altered the entire cast of his features. "If you're right, I'm as sound as I ever was!

"Exactly," Bryce asserted. "That's the point, the thing we've been tryin' to hammer into you, Lamb. It's the kernel in the nut."

Lamb set his teeth. The muscles tensed in his cheeks till they showed as tightly knotted bundles. "But—this—drug?" he questioned, thickly.

"Something which could be given to you gradually, and, once it had produced its intended effect, as gradually removed," I said.

He stared into my face. His own was white, set, with those little corded muscle still bulging in his cheeks. "By God, I believe you mean it!" he suddenly rasped.

"Of course we mean it!" Something akin to exasperation sounded in Jim's voice. "An' we're askin' you to give us a chance to prove it. What's the matter? Don't you fancy the notion, or what?"

"Fancy it?" Suddenly Imer Lamb swayed, sank into a chair, and covered his face with his hands. I saw their fingers quiver. "Fancy it! Lord, if you knew what it means—what it means to me! It's nothing short of a pardon to a condemned man, the difference between life and death. It means life if it's true. Life—life—" His voice sank to a whisper and trailed off. He sat staring straight before him. It was as though he gazed into a future his final words had conjured up.

"That you let us prove it true, Mr. Lamb, is all we ask," I broke the ensuing silence. "We bring you the invitation from a man who stands ready to explain everything that has happened. He asks you to accept, and Miss Mason asks it. Last night you refused her, but can you refuse her again today—this request of hers that you go with us and grasp the opportunity to be convinced?"

"You know that, do you, that I refused her?" he asked as I paused.

I nodded. "She told us this morning, Mr. Lamb. And she's worked for you—your interests all through this matter—worked. Now—"

"Oh, I'm going with you." He stood up. At last I read belief in his eyes. "I want to be convinced—want to, do you understand me? But this thing is a shock. It staggered me, shook me up. I wasn't expecting it. But now—" He broke off.

There was a sound of a heavy hand hammering against the door of the suite.

"Excuse me a moment," Lamb said, and went to open the door.

"Imer!" Bryce and I heard the sound of a heavy, excited masculine voice. "You're here! Thank the Lord! See here. I've got to see you, got to see you alone! I've just come from Moira."

I glanced at Jim. I recognized the speaker despite his shaken tones, and I found recognition in my partner's face.

Then Imer Lamb was speaking. "Well, just a minute, George. What the deuce is the matter with you?"

"I tell you I've got to see you, got to see you now," his foster brother replied. "I was afraid I might miss you."

"Just a minute," Imer stayed him. "Come in here." He closed the door and led George Lamb into the room where we sat. "I have visitors, George—Messrs. Glace and Bryce. Gentlemen, my brother, George Lamb."

"Er—yes. Glace and Bryce?" George Lamb was disheveled. He was perspiring freely; his collar was a wilted thing about his heavy neck; his face was actually livid as he turned his eyes upon us. "Er—glad to meet you gentlemen—again."

"Again?" Quickly Imer Lamb appeared to seize on the word. "Oh, so you've met them before then, have you, George?"

"Yes—yes," the brother said thickly. "Yes, Imer, I've met them. But see here—I've got something to tell you."

"Suppose I know it already?" As he spoke I saw a full conviction form on Imer Lamb's face. It looked from between his narrowed lids as they marked his brother's perturbation. It sounded in his voice as he repeated: "Suppose I know it already, George?"

And that quiet, almost accusing question left George Lamb puzzled; I could see that too. A half-frown formed on his sweating brow. "Know it already," he stammered, and then, as understanding came upon him. "You mean these two here told you, Glace and Bryce? You mean they were wise, came here to wise you up?"

Imer Lamb nodded his head. He smiled, but there was not the slightest hint of humor in his act. Rather I thought it was the acceptance of a fact, the surrender of the last shred of unbelief, a sad thing that marked the final relinquishment of a faltering hope.

"As a matter of fact, George, they did come to see me about it," he said. "They came to ask me to go with them to a man who has been an unknown friend, while one I should have had every right to trust seems to have lent himself as partner to a rotten scheme against me."

"Semi Dual, you mean Semi Dual!" George Lamb fairly shouted. "You mean their sidekick with the funny name sent 'em to you?" Guilt set its mark upon him as he stood there. It was in his entire bearing; it was in his voice.

I glanced at Bryce. There was no question now but that George Lamb, true to his Uranian nature, had blown up. He stood there self-convicted by his guilty knowledge mirrored in his own words. And Moira Mason, Bo-Peep, had sent him. He had said so. She had followed Dual's directions, and this was the result.

I felt Imer Lamb's glance upon me, met it, and nodded slightly. It shifted back to his brother. And then he spoke: "I didn't know his name before. They didn't tell me. But I am going to hear what he has to say about it. I had agreed to go before you got here. Hadn't you better come along?"

The thing was more than a question; it was a command, a challenge. Imer Lamb, the man who had been an American "ace," who had within the last few days won himself the title of the "Mad Aviator" by his aerial antics, had regained control of himself. And George Lamb seemed to feel it.

"Imer—" he said hoarsely.

"I think you had better go with us, George," his foster brother cut him off. "Very well, gentlemen. Suppose we start. Really it seems scarcely necessary now, so far as I am concerned; but common courtesy could scarcely dictate less."

"Imer—I've hardly time," George Lamb began as Bryce and I rose. "I've quite a bit to attend to this afternoon. You—"

"Oh, if I was you I wouldn't bother telling Nathalia, George." Jim's suggestion cut off his words. "If you did she might tell that precious brother of hers that you'd spilled the beans, just like she probably told you what I said to her the other day on the street."

"Brother?" Imer Lamb stiffened.

"Nathalia Norton is Dr. Drake's sister," I advised.

"George?" he swung back to the broker. Comprehension, sorrow, and something like loathing were in his face.

George Lamb hung his head. His bearing became that of a chided culprit. He made no effort to meet his brother's eyes.

Imer's jaw set again in decision. "Well, George, now more than ever I think you had best go with us. Come, gentlemen," he said.

CHAPTER XIX

THE SHOW-DOWN

WE LEFT THE suite, and descended to where our taxi waited. The four of us entered the machine. I told the driver to take us back to the Urania. We were off.

George Lamb sat slumped down in his seat; there was a certain spineless quality, about his heavy-set figure that spoke of an inward collapse. His former forceful, blustering demeanor had vanished. He did not speak.

Nor did Imer Lamb speak either as we ran back to the heart of the city. Now and then I saw his glance turn to George, the man whom as a boy his father had taken, adopted, treated in every way as his own child, the man who had requited such treatment in the way it now appeared he had.

Bryce lighted a cigar and smoked. I leaned back and waited. This was the end, I thought, of the strange, well-nigh invisible course the whole affair had run until now at the last, when things were to be explained, the picture was to be built up, by Semi Dual, the one who throughout it all had marked its veiled progress from first to last by the steady onward sweep on the face of the Clock of the Skies.

The cab fought through the traffic, edged into the curb before the Urania, and stopped. We got out, paid our driver, went into the lofty foyer, and entered a cage.

On the twentieth floor I led my companions out, and along the tiled corridor to the bronze-and-marble stairs.

At their foot, Imer Lamb paused. I saw a quick comprehension in his face.

"Up here?" he questioned.

And when I nodded, went on. "This friend of yours is up here? I say, Glace, when I've been flying over, you know, I've seen something that looked like a garden on the roof."

"It is," I told him, realizing how well he might have marked it from his plane, little dreaming even so what it was.

We climbed the stairs, and came out at the top. The chimes rang out in the tower. Imer Lamb smiled with a fleeting appreciation of the beauty of that unexpected spot in the heart of the milling city, of the roses, the fountain where gray and white doves were preening themselves on the basin. I heard George Lamb draw a rasping breath.

Then we were at the tower, and Henri was bowing slightly as he spoke in greeting: "Welcome, friends of the master. He awaits your coming. You are the last."

"Henri!" Imer Lamb exclaimed.

"M. Lamb," Henri returned. "One follows orders, *monsieur*. I trust *monsieur* understands."

"Oh, quite." Imer nodded. We crossed the anteroom, passed the door of the room beyond, and paused.

I myself, I may as well confess it, was surprised. Dual sat by his desk as was his custom, clad in his white and purple robes. But the room was otherwise occupied. Marya Harding, Moira Mason and Haddon, debonair and smiling, I saw; and Johnson, heavy-set, stolidly waiting, and Gladys Ashton, come forth now as it seemed from her period of recuperation in Marya's house, and Simpson, who nodded as his eyes met mine, and Joe Kingsley, who, as we appeared and as he saw his friend and former employer, half started from his seat, and sank back again with his eyes never shifting from his face.

It was quite a jury before which, as I saw now, Semi Dual was to present the evidence in this matter which had in greater or less degree involved each in its course.

He rose. "Welcome, Mr. Imer Lamb," he said "whom though I have never met before in the flesh I have come to know in a different fashion through those methods which it is given me to use. Welcome, since now it is come time for us to meet, and review the records of those things which have been, but which now are happily past."

Imer Lamb bowed. "I thank you, sir," he made answer. "And you will pardon me if I do not fully understand as yet. But I have brought my brother with me. It appeared to me that it was best." He glanced at George.

"A needless precaution, but one which can alter nothing in the further course of this matter," Semi Dual replied.

"So?" The word was a question. And as he spoke, I saw Imer Lamb's eyes run to Moira Mason, who sat on a heavily-cushioned couch. There was a place beside her, and he went toward it as the rest of us found seats.

Dual picked up his auditors with his glance, "We are complete." He began speaking again in his bell-like voice, that in that moment some way reminded me of the intonations of a priest—a priest of justice, I thought, a priest of right, of high principle, integrity, truth—as he stood there in his vestments.

"We are complete," he repeated, "save only Saturn, Neptune and Mars; Neptune who brought this matter to an issue, and Mars who carried out those things which Neptune designed. Yet are Neptune and Mars foredoomed to be smitten with the fiery sword of the Sun now that their scheming has led them within the path of its destroying arc.

"And I to that end have assembled you here that you may understand how selfishness, treachery, double-dealing, disregard of the rights of others, greed, avarice, lust may bring the undoing of those who employ them, about.

"In the beginning, my friends, I am one who reads the stars. Men's lives are a complex of influences of an electro-magnetic nature even as man's life is an electromagnetic thing, as science dominates the invisible, ceaselessly active electromagnetic quality of which all matter is composed.

"Viewed so, my friends, each planet is but a center of electromagnetic force, of a quality polarized to itself, a quality which each radiates, the one to the other endlessly, And those radiations from one planet to another endlessly affect each of the material force forms which it supports.

"Hence man's life is affected by the combined radiations active at the moment of his birth, and the further course of his life is, as we may say, polarized. Wherefore if one knows the hour of a man's birth and the position of the planets, the stars at that hour, then may one predicate upon that basis the events of that man's life. Am I clear?" He glanced at Imer Lamb.

He inclined his head as he sat beside Bo-Peep. There was a tiny frown of concentration on his forehead.

"Then to the practical demonstration." Semi Dual smiled. "In the beginning, Mr. Lamb, I set up a figure of the happening at Monk's Hall on the night when your affliction came upon you in full force, the influences of the actions of others against you, and the course of your life came as it were to a head. For no man lives to himself alone, my friends. The lives of this one and that one overlap, interlock. The life of another meeting yours may wholly alter it. So it is written, and experience proves it truth.

"Also I erected astrological figures for the natal dates of you, Mr. Lamb, and of the woman beside you now, Miss Moira Mason, who brought the entire matter to my notice first. And I found your Mercury and your Moon afflicted by Saturn, by Neptune, by Mars, and by Uranus. And remember that each planet holds a quality of its own, a quality designed to produce certain effects. Saturn in this case would incline to nervous and mental conditions, epilepsy by day, insanity by night, perhaps."

Moira Mason gasped. The sound whispered through the room.

"You attacked your valet, Joseph Kingsley, at night, Mr. Lamb," Dual continued. "So much for that. Neptune rules drugs which strongly affect the nerves. Mars rules tobacco among drugs. It was this connection which made me first suspicious of the method employed against you when I learned that you smoked overmuch. Neptune and Mars both evilly posited to your Mercury and Moon might well indicate that your tobacco was blended with a reason-destroying adulterant."

Again a sound ran through the room, and turned all eyes on George Lamb where he sat, sheer horror and consternation on his face. It was not an articulate thing. It was more a groan, raucous, all-confessing, hoarse.

"Wait," Dual spoke into the tensely ensuing silence that marked that self-betraying audition. "Wait, Uranus. Thou, too, wast evilly posited to thy brother's Mercury and Moon, and before this meeting is finished each planet I have named shall be identified as an individual present, or one who if not present still played his or her part.

"From what I have said then, the case of Imer Lamb were hopeless, save that Venus, Jupiter, and the Sun throw their friendly rays toward his Mercury and Moon to give him aid. In this was his salvation which led me to predicate his full return to a normal mental balance in time, a time which has now arrived. And so to redeem a promise. I, Jupiter, have watched this matter from the beginning.

"Jupiter is the arbiter, the judge; Jupiter is justice, who shall see justice done. Jupiter marks, watches, waits. And in this matter, Miss Moira Mason is Venus. Let Venus speak."

All eyes turned on Bo-Peep as Semi paused.

"I—was terribly troubled when Mr. Lamb was arrested," she began her narrative. "And I went to Marya Harding, and she knew Mr. Dual and brought me to him, and he agreed to do all he could.

"Then when Mr. Lamb was paroled to his brother I came and asked him if I couldn't get a special attendant for him, and he sent his own companion to be with him in that House of Invisible Bondage as he called Dr. Drake's place.

"He went by his orders, and he watched, and one day Henri found an address in a waste paper basket in Dr. Drake's study, as Mr. Dual told me afterward. Then Dr. Drake told me I ought to go away; that it would be better for Imer if I were not here when he was released."

"Moira!" Imer Lamb whispered harshly.

She turned her eyes to him briefly, and smiled. "I told Mr. Dual about that, and he told me to go to Los Angeles. And he told me to try and learn what I could about Dr. Drake who had practiced there before he came here, and about Miss Nathalie Norton who had been a motion picture actress some years ago.

"And he gave me this address Henri had found in the waste-paper basket, and told me that a man would call on me after I got to Los Angeles, and I should give it to him. So I went, although I hated to, because I felt it would seem very strange to Imer if I was, gone when he got out.

"But Mr. Dual told me that by doing what he asked I could help Imer most. And maybe I did, because I found out that Dr. Drake had left Los Angeles because he had got into trouble there, and that Miss Norton is really his sister, Nathalie Drake, and Mr. Haddon, who is here today, hunted up the address of this man Henri found.

"It was the address of a Mexican; he placed him under arrest after it was found he was raising and selling a certain drug. You see, the address Henri found was on the wrapper of a package of drugs Dr. Drake received from Los Angeles. And then I came back."

"And from the first," Dual's voice came again before any one could speak in comment, "it was written that Venus should greatly aid. And what is to be will be, my friends. Herein as applying to Venus it stands verified.

"Yet if one studies the conjoined charts of Imer Lamb and Venus one sees that the end is not yet, but that in the future as in that which is now past she shall aid him, should he keep her with him, and make her the influence in his life for which in every way she is fit."

"Moira!" Imer Lamb whispered once more.

She turned to him, reached out, and covered his hand with hers.

He drew it into his.

"And now, Henri," Semi prompted. "You have played a part, indicated already, yet not wholly."

"The straw-gatherer," Bryce mumbled to me as Henri rose and advanced.

"The master sent me as Miss Mason has said," he declared. "And I went. *Certainment.* I went, an' I watched. I was all eyes, all ears. I heard things; I saw things. My suspicion was intense. I found the address as it is said I found it. Antonio Moreno—"

"Saturn," Dual broke in to announce. "Saturn, a raiser and marketer of the drug, a drug many Mexicans mix with tobacco and smoke, a reason—destroying, murder—inducing drug which even robs the murderer of a recollection of the act after he has recovered from its influence. And did not Saturn afflict the Mercury and Moon of Mr. Lamb through the effects of the drug he raised? Proceed, my friend."

"I found it as already stated," Henri resumed. "But I did something else. *Mon Dieu,* yes. As a spy I was a success. I found that the woman Nathalie Norton came often to the house. I found another woman—this young woman who sits here, Miss Gladys Ashton. I found she was being detained as a prisoner.

"Oh, yes. She told me of her uncle who was paying to have her kept there. I learned her date of birth. I carried it to the master, and in the stars he read the truth that she was being held there without need, and being given drugs. Also I discovered that Dr. Drake mixed something with tobacco, and gave it to those in his house who smoked, and I managed to gather a little of that tobacco into my possession, and bring it to the master.

"Also I went to see Imer Lamb's valet who was at his rooms. That was easy; I was now M. Lamb's attendant. I called at his rooms, and we had a talk. In the course of it I discovered I had no tobacco, and this valet of his kindly supplied me out of a quantity his master had left. But I smoked not all of it—oh, no. It, too, I brought to the master. And in both instances it contained the drug.

"But that was not all. I listened as I have said, and I discovered what was in the life chart of Miss Ashton also, a danger to her life. It was a plot to destroy her I overheard, between— this Norton woman and Dr. Drake. Her uncle was financially ruined, what you call broke. No longer could he pay, and she knew too much of what went on in that house. So then I helped her escape. That is all of importance. *C'est fini.*"

It was all matching up, all working out. Step by step everything was coming now to the surface as each star, each planet, actually present, they or their satellites, those who had aided them in all that had been, step by step described his or her part.

It was a bit weird, a bit odd, to sit there, and hear each speak as though a star itself had for the moment been endowed with a human voice, to see the picture growing so complete that one even saw how it had not mattered that Drake took away the evidence of the tobacco Kingsley had not smoked before Imer Lamb was released.

"And now," said Semi Dual as Henri retired, "I shall ask Miss Gladys Ashton to take up the story which can but prove how the thread of one human life is interwoven with yet other lives. No man lives to himself alone.

"And had not Imer Lamb entered the House of Invisible Bondage those things Henri has described as affecting her might well not have been discovered—and if not, she had died.

"Yet today she is with us to furnish a further demonstration of how in selfishness, in blind self-seeking, are contained the fatal causes by which a man may be destroyed."

He ceased, and Gladys Ashton fumbled in a little bead bag on her lap. From it she drew a letter, and held it in her hand as she told her story, sketching those facts I have already narrated until the time Bryce and I had left her at Marya Harding's house.

"I've been there ever since," she said, "until today, when Inspector Johnson came and said Mr. Dual had sent him, and that I was to go with him to my uncle's attorneys in the Stroller Building. Marya and I went with him, and they gave me a letter, and I brought it with me. I'll read it, if you like."

"Read it, Gladys," Semi prompted.

And she nodded, drew several sheets of closely written paper from the envelope she held, and began:

> My dear niece:
>
> I am a condemned man. My fellow men would condemn me if they knew, and I condemn myself. I am a cheat—a thief, and worse. I can write it down, because when you read it I shall be beyond any human law. I shall kill myself tonight.
>
> Gladys, at the time your mother died I was in desperate financial straits. And you were a child in experience in such matters as I knew, and in a state unfitting you for any cool judgment as a result of your mother's death. I came to you, and you know the rest.
>
> I met Dr. Drake—quite accidentally at that time—and mentioned your nervous condition, and he suggested that he see you. At that time, I swear, I had not thought of what I afterward did. But I did get you to give me a power of attorney, meaning to use what I needed of your money, and replace it later, the false hope of the gambler always.
>
> You will recall that your mother transferred her property to you before her death to avoid the necessity of probate proceedings. No one was concerned about it save you, and I, who needed money so badly, and the State, to whom an inheritance tax was due.
>
> I paid the inheritance tax out of your property, of course, and what few bills that were incurred as a result of your mother's illness and death. This done, I had a free hand, with you out of the way.
>
> It was Drake who suggested how easy it would be to keep you in his place. I don't know, but I think he had an inkling that

things were going badly with me. Be that as it may, I agreed to his unholy scheme to keep you a prisoner, and use your money in my constantly failing efforts to recoup each succeeding loss.

For I lost, Gladys, I lost, lost—always I lost. I am a broken man. I made a prisoner of you, Gladys, and then I made a prisoner of myself to Drake. He bled me white. His demands grew and grew, and I had to meet them; I dared not refuse—until I could no longer meet them.

Then he—he is a fiend—he hinted that sometimes those in his institution grew sick, and died; and then he called me, and told me you had escaped. And I do not know—I may be a murderer, Gladys; this may never meet your eyes. I may have killed you, been the cause of your death at least.

And so I am taking the one way out. There is a little something left, I think—not much, but maybe enough to keep you from want, if you still are alive. Heaven grant it that you are alive, and that it will prove enough. It is the last prayer of one who has wronged and betrayed every human trust he should have kept inviolate, before he goes to meet his God.

Your uncle,
John Parkins.

"That's all," Gladys Ashton said as she folded it up. "It's—very sad."

"Good told me today that as far as he could tell the money end of that prayer was apt to be answered, though he couldn't say how far," Johnson said, speaking for the first time.

Moira Mason wiped her eyes.

It was another bit in the story. It was an odd posthumous sort of revenge John Parkins had taken on the man who had persuaded him into his clutches, and then blackmailed him to the last. I let my eyes run about the room. There was understanding, and a sort of grim anticipation on each face I met. And there was a sort of growing horror on the face of George Lamb where he sat.

"And now, Mr. Haddon," Semi prompted.

Haddon nodded. "That helps to check up this end of it," he

replied. "As for my end, there isn't much. Mr. Dual located me, and wired me to look up Miss Mason in Los Angeles. I did so. She gave me an address. It was that of a Mexican who had a little truck farm, a market garden. But along with the other stuff he was raising was a patch of this marihuana—"

CHAPTER XX

MARIHUANA

"MARIHUANA!" BRYCE ERUPTED gruffly.

"Marihuana, yes, Mr. Bryce," Semi said, "a drug which produces a homicidal mania in those who indulge in its continued use, the drug which was found in the tobacco my friend and trusted companion Henri obtained both from the rooms of Mr. Imer Lamb, and from Dr. Hugo Drake's house. Pardon the interruption, Mr. Haddon."

"I think the fact is sufficient, and is appreciated by every one present. Antonio Moreno was arrested, and incidentally a letter to him from Dr. Hugo Drake was intercepted. That letter was answered to the effect that no further supply of the drug could be forwarded at the present, and Antonio signed it to that effect at my request." Once more Haddon smiled.

"An' after he got that letter Drake turned loose a couple of other patients besides Lamb!" Jim exclaimed in sudden comprehension of what might have lain back of the fact he announced, a sudden shortage in the supply of the subtle drug Drake was using, the drug that rendered and kept men insane.

"And perchance he deemed it best to do so, once Miss Ashton had escaped beyond his control, and he knew not her whereabouts," Semi said. "As to him, and, his institution of illegal and dishonest practice Dr. Simpson has still more information to give."

Simpson nodded. He cleared his throat. "Both illegal and dishonest," he declared. "Dr. Dual, after we had met, asked me what I knew about Drake, and I told him little except that he was unpopular with the regular profession. But even so, I never suspected the truth of what was going on right under our eyes until following my first conversation with Dr. Dual. I determined to investigate.

"Then it wasn't long until I had uncovered Drake, and was ready to proceed against him any time our friend here gave the word. Putting it briefly, Drake isn't any more a doctor than one of these fakers that used to stand around the corners with a banjo player under a gasoline torch, while they peddled patent lotions and pills.

"The school he claims to have graduated from is a school all right, but he never graduated, let alone attended it. His diploma is a forged document. Dr. Hugo Drake, as he calls himself, is a diploma-mill graduate. It was easy enough for me to find out from the registrar of Waburn College.

"His name does not appear on his lists of either graduates or matriculates, but you know what a tear-up there was about this diploma-mill business, and I ran out that part of it. Some of the people arrested in connection with that business kept records of their own, and Drake's name is on one of those. Well, that fixes his standing as a 'doctor,' and, of course, makes illegal any professional work he attempts in this State."

"Wherein once more a man's double-dealing has, like an uncertain tool, turned in his hand against him," Semi said as Simpson ceased.

I glanced at Jim, and saw he understood. Not merely to care for Gladys Ashton had Semi contrived his meeting with Simpson, but to inspire him to investigate Drake's professional standing, which as both an accredited member of the profession, and a man in touch with the police of the city he very easily could. He met my glance, and nodded in what I took for comprehension.

Dual's voice went on: "Thus, my friends, the picture grows; thus is its every light and shadow brought out. It is not a pleasant picture, this; yet thus was it painted by those responsible for it in their own acts. Joseph Kingsley, have you perhaps something to add to it?"

Joe Kingsley rose, and came a step or two forward with his halting walk. To me it seemed that he did so in order that as he spoke be might still keep his eyes on Imer Lamb's face.

"Hi 'aven't much to sye," he began in his cockney fashion. "But Hi ain't goin' to pass the chance to sye a word. Hit's a rum go—ha rum go. Though Hi didn't know 'arf 'ow rum hit was till Doc Simpson 'ere told me arfter Hi was in th' county 'orspital, w'ere Hi've been since.

"But 'es a w'ite man, Doc Simpson, an' Mr. Dual 'ere, 'e's a prince. Arfter that Hi seen hit, hof course. Arfter Mr. Himer was took away Hi did smoke that baccy, never dreaming there was hanythink wrong with the stuff. Gor blyme, there waren't nuthin' to do but smoke. Hi smoked hand looked arfter 'is things, hand took 'em hover 'ere to Drake's, as 'e needed 'em fill the day w'en Drake come hand arsked me for what was left of the baccy hand said Hi was fired, 'cause hit wouldn't be good for Mr. Himer to 'ave me around arfter 'e was turned hout."

"He told you that did he, Joe?" Imer Lamb asked quickly.

"Ho, yus, sir." Kingsley nodded. "Them was halmost 'is very words."

"And they told me you'd left me, Joe, after I was out and asked about you, told me you'd left because you were afraid—"

"W'at's that?" Kingsley shouted. "Hafraid, sir—me, w'o did me bit in the war, w'o never turned tail yet—afraid? Why, Gorblast their bloody, rotten 'earts for bleatin' liars!"

"Here, here," Imer stayed him. "They did lie, Joe, but it's all right now. You're coming back, old fellow; you're coming back, aren't you?"

"Ham I?" The two men looked upon one another. "You're jolly well right Hi ham, sir, hand thankin' you for th' chance." And suddenly with a touch of the dramatic I had not expected, he drew himself up, soldierwise at attention, and snapped through a hand salute.

And Imer Lamb returned it before Kingsley hobbled back to his seat. Some way it brought a sudden tightness, a sudden ache into my throat.

And then again Dual was speaking again: "And now, thou Uranus. Thus have the friendly planets, the friendly satellites of those planets, those who aided them in their troubles or their endeavors, spoken save only my two friends, Glace and Bryce. Yet have they worked under my personal direction and their words could but duplicate those we have already heard.

"But thou—thou are of those who have threatened in the life chart of the man I have considered, yea even from the first. And thou art here among us since now, as I think the evil influence of thy position in this matter has run out, even as perchance the evil of thy first intent has within the past few days drained from thy heart. You have sat among us, and heard what has been said. Say thou then whether truly or falsely have those who have spoken borne witness. Speak, Uranus, speak."

George Lamb stirred. The attention of every one in the room was focused upon him in a flash. He lifted his head, His face was a sickly pallor, the whites of his eyes showed reddened between their lids. "There isn't much I can say. Most of it's been said already. I'm guilty," he began with a visible effort at last, "though Heaven knows this thing went a lot farther than I meant it should when I went into it.

"Some of what's been said I knew, and some of it I did not. All I meant to do really was to keep Imer from marrying. That's the truth. You know his money as well as mine is in our business, and if he died without an heir, why, I'd inherit it, or if I dropped off first it would be his. So—"

"So that was it, was it?" Imer interrupted. "Well, you would have got it this afternoon if this conference hadn't come up. Hard luck, George—hard luck!"

"Don't!" Suddenly George Lamb whimpered. "I didn't want it, that way. I didn't want it. I don't want it, damn it!"

His voice cracked, broke. "I didn't, I tell you. I've proved it. I went to Moira last night, and told her she'd got to stop you, and today again I went to her after she telephoned me she'd failed, and told her to marry you, do anything to keep you from goin, up this afternoon in any more of those fool flying stunts of yours.

"I told her—begged her to marry you; I all but went down on my knees. And she sent me to you, and I came. That's how I come to be here. I came to tell you, stop you—confess." He broke off, and sat panting like one who had run a long distance.

"And how," came the voice of Semi Dual, "did you come also to think of the plan you put into operation first?"

Lamb turned his bloodshot eyes to him. "I didn't," he declared. "I—just told Na—a friend of mine—"

"Hugo Drake's sister, your intimate friend." Semi forced the issue upon him.

He nodded. "Yes. I told Nathalie about Imer's engagement, and said I wished there was some way to keep him from marrying Moira or anybody else. And she—she suggested that she talk things over with her brother. You know the rest.

"He told me it could be done without permanent damage to Imer, that he would furnish me the tobacco already mixed with the drug. I told Imer about the new blend I had discovered, and I smoked it too; I really did, only mine wasn't mixed with the stuff like his.

"I got him to try it, and he liked it, and then the rest happened and everything seemed working out all right, though Glace and Bryce here did come to see me, and afterwards Bryce stopped Nathalie on the street, and it worried me a bit.

"Drake didn't like Imer having a special attendant either. But Mrs. Harding and Moira insisted, and there didn't seem to be any reasonable way for us to refuse, and we didn't think any one could really suspect.

"You see, Drake had got onto the stuff when he was in California, and we fancied it safe. Our plan was to get Imer off it while Drake had him, and then to turn him loose after telling him he was all right unless his trouble should recur. We figured that would keep him from marrying.

"I knew him—I knew he wouldn't take a chance on marriage, on having children with—a thing like that hanging over his head. But when he started trying to commit suicide in that plane of his I blew up. I hadn't counted on that. I ain't a Cain— and I wasn't trying to kill him; I didn't want him to be killed. I didn't—as the Lord is my witness!"

"Nay," said Semi Dual, "I do not think so, nor have I thought so. Wherefore I have not included you in those against whom the law shall take its course—save only the higher law which says that by a man's actions shall he be judged, under which, as it chances, a man ofttimes judges himself to the end that he continueth in the path he has followed, or deciding it unworthy, decides further to alter his course. But Saturn, Neptune and Mars—"

Through the course of the whole proceeding from the time he had greeted Imer Lamb he had been seated. Now he rose as a judge might rise in passing sentence.

"Saturn already in durance, and Neptune, poisoner of men's minds, ruler of poisonous drugs. Neptune, Nathalie Norton, Nathalie Drake, the adventuress. Neptune secretive, scheming, crafty, who in this affair stands as the guilty one—the primal cause, who devised this plan to dethrone a man's reason if no more than for a time, that she might profit by it perchance, who conceived this unholy plan by which a man was turned against his benefactor's child, debauching others and herself debauched.

"Neptune and Mars who aided and abetted her in her treacherous scheming; against them the Sun, which is the law in this affair, shall strike with a flaming sword; the law of man as well as the law of God shall take its course. Mr. Johnson—"

Johnson stiffened as his name rang out. It was as though he came to attention at a commanding voice.

"And you, Mr. Haddon—"

Haddon nodded. His lips twitched in a faintly comprehending smile.

"You are the law in this matter. Go; do your duty. Lay hands upon this guilty Mars and Neptune, brother and sister in iniquity as in the flesh, go seize them and haul them before the bar of justice, that the law may have its will of them, because of their unlawful acts. Go now, at once. They are waiting for you; they shall not escape, inasmuch as since the day when Antonio Morena, Saturn, was apprehended without their knowing they have been watched."

Watched? Now I understood the smile that still lingered on Haddon's lips. That had been a part of his participation. He had provided against Drake or his sister succeeding in any endeavor to escape. They had been watched by unseen eyes, their every move marked. It was so the Federal service worked.

Johnson was on his feet. Haddon got up. They were men assigned to an errand; one felt it would be carried out. They were men, but it seemed they were more than that. They were the Sun, the Law, the visible, tangible symbols of an eternal, never to be escaped force, a power as eternal as the stars themselves by which the mandates of the law were carried out.

"All right then, we'll get 'em," Johnson's voice came gruffly in a pledge of a mission to be fulfilled. "Good afternoon, folks."

Followed by Haddon, unruffled, still slightly smiling, he stalked out.

A sigh ran through the room, a relaxing of tension, a release of half-bated breathing. It was as though now at the end of the past hour, we who still sat there were slipping back into the normal grooves, the normal channels of everyday life.

For this was the climax. We had met, we had spoken together, and the verdict had been reached. The Sun, toward the carrying out of that verdict, had gone forth to strike.

Soon that House of Invisible Bondage in which the slaves of an invisible bondage had been held chained by unlawful means, doubly enslaved by a crafty, conscienceless schemer, would be as though it had never been. Its unholy secret, its invisible menace, was at last unveiled.

Imer Lamb sat here beside woman he loved, the woman of his choice, his mate. He had been freed from that invisible bondage which others had forced upon him by means of an illicit drug. This then was the end.

And once more Semi's voice: "Wherefore, Venus, here is the ending, and the beginning. For as the present runs imperceptibly into the past, so does the future melt ever imperceptibly into the present, and what the future shall be depends wholly upon what we make of it in the present. Man is exalted or destroyed by his own just or unjust acts."

And as though his words were a signal for dismissal, those he had gathered together looked not at him, but at one another, stirred, shifted, and rose.

"Joe," I heard Imer Lamb speaking, "go on over to the rooms and stick around. I'll be back sometime, and we'll have a jolly good talk." He tossed a bunch of keys to Kingsley, who caught them and went out with a smile upon his face.

Henri went with him.

Simpson glanced at his watch, shook hands with Dual and left.

Then Marya was speaking to Semi. I caught her words: "You're just the same—just the same as you were; you never change. You're as immutable, as sure, as right as your own stars."

"Because I read them, Marya, friend," I heard him answer.

And then. "Well, Bo-Peep, you got your Lamb back, but—after listenin' to what's been said, I dunno—looks more like he'd been a goat." Jim's voice boom out as he crossed to where Moira and Imer stood.

Imer Lamb frowned slightly, uncomprehendingly, and Moira laughed.

"Oh, Mr. Bryce calls me Bo-Peep, because she lost her sheep, you know, Imer. And I rather like the fancy."

And then she turned to Jim. "Just so, I've got him again, Mr.

Bryce, I don't care what he is. And now I've got him I'm going to keep him." Her fingers curled themselves in a possessive way on Imer's arm.

I heard a lagging footfall behind me, half turned, and looked into the bloodshot eyes of his foster brother.

"Imer?" he said thickly.

Imer turned his head, but did not answer.

"Imer," George Lamb repeated. "I—I just want to tell you I'm glad. I've lived in hell the last few weeks. I got into it, boy—and I couldn't get out. I had to go through. They had me where they wanted me, Imer. I think maybe they meant to keep me where they wanted me, if this hadn't turned out as it did—just like they kept Parkins where they wanted him till he killed himself. So I'm glad, boy, glad, and I'd like to be best man."

"George!" Imer's voice was grating, harsh, yet even so, a bit unsteady.

"Oh, Imer, let him," Moira pleaded, with a sound half sob, half laughter, in the words.

We stood in a well of silence. Without our realizing it, the voices of those around us had ceased. Then into it Semi's words dropped plummet like:

"Let her guide you, her by whose efforts you are saved. Let her guide you now, and in the future. She will not lead you astray, so that you let her hold you in the bonds of love. For love is truly the activating, motivating force of the universe itself. Only those who deny it are destroyed."

"It won't be difficult. It won't be difficult." Imer Lamb looked down deep into the lifted blue eyes of the girl who raised them to his. And then he laughed out, shrugged like a man who casts a clogging weight from his shoulders, and turned again to his brother.

"All right, George," he said.

DR. HUGO DRAKE, NATHALIE NORTON ARRESTED

Once more the headlines flared the following morning. And the minute I got to the office Jim came in with the paper, of course.

"Well, they got them, I see," I said.

"Got 'em. Of course they got 'em. Them two was slated for gettin'," he declared.

I nodded. It is hard indeed for the guilty to escape when the Law, the Sun, turns the light of his vengeance upon them, and strikes with a flaming sword.

ABOUT THE AUTHOR: DR. J.U. GIESY

BORN NEAR CHILLICOTHE, Ohio, August 6, 1877. That makes me a Buckeye, and some people have suggested that I was a nut. Of my actual birth I have no recollection. So this is mere hearsay evidence. When I was eight months of age my parents removed to southeastern Kansas and took me with them, as I was still unable to shift for myself.

When I was thirteen we again removed to Utah, where I received my common school education in common with other youngsters of a similar age. In 1895, I entered the Starling Medical College, Columbus, Ohio, and received my medical degree from that institution in 1898.

Returning to Salt Lake, I served an internship in a local hospital and have practiced medicine in that city ever since, with the exception of the time I spent in the United States service during the World War as a captain in the Medical Corps. As regards the Army I am still a major in the Reserve, attached to the Division Surgeon's Office of the 104th Division. In 1916 I was instrumental in organizing the first Plattsburg camp ever held in the State, starting the movement and acting as secretary of the general committee which put it over.

I began to write in 1910. Unlike many well known writers, I have had rejections since. At the same time I've found a lot of editors who liked my work. I have written as an avocation ever since. At present I am associate editor for Utah on the staff of *California and Western Medicine*, and the staff of the

Archives of Physical Therapy X-Ray and Radium. Because of the latter fact I am a member of the American Medical Editors Association.

I am also a member of the Salt Lake Chamber of Commerce, and a life member of the American College of Physical Therapy, which I have served as an officer for several years. My ancestors made me a Son of the American Revolution, and I have made myself more or less of a nuisance to a lot of people all by myself.

J.U. Giesy

I was married in San Francisco, to Juliet Galena Conwell, in December, 1904, and the marriage took. Personally I think they did better work along those lines, that long ago. Anyway we're still living in the same apartment, with no intentions of divorce.

Just why the editor should want to print this confession I really can't imagine. But that's his business. He's asked for it and here it is!

ABOUT THE AUTHOR: JUNIUS B. SMITH

I WAS BORN at Salt Lake City, Utah, September 29, 1883, at approximately 3:55:27 P.M., right ascension of the mid-heaven (for the benefit of my astrological readers) 16 hrs. 27 min. 57 sec., or 246° 59' 15"; position of planets, Neptune 20° 45' ret. Taurus, Saturn 10° 6' ret. Gemini, Mars 22° 10' Cancer, Jupiter 0° 26' Leo, Moon 22° 24' Virgo, Uranus 24° 34' Virgo, Sun 6° 27' 23" Libra, Venus 8° 52' Libra, Mercury 20° 31' ret. Libra. Declinations: Sun 2° 34' south, Moon 0° 7' south, Neptune 16° 13' north, Uranus 2° 50' north, Saturn 20° 2' north, Jupiter 20° 18' north, Mars 22° 25' north, Venus 2° 20' south, Mercury 11° 17' south.

With this meager astronomical data, the astrologians will know more about me than I could write in a volume.

For the benefit of you other readers:

I am an attorney at law and practiced for many years, paying my office expenses in the lean years by writing. I never had the bitter experience of having to write years before anything sold. At the beginning of my writing career, Dr. J.U. Giesy and I joined intellectual forces, and our first joint effort was submitted to *Argosy* way back in 1911. It sold, first time out. Rapidly we "dashed" off more and they sold also. We each write separately as well as jointly, at such times as we cannot get together.

Early in life I took up astrology as a hobby and lived to see it recognized in judicial decisions as a science. That I have helped, in some measure, to brush away the misconceptions in the minds of many people regarding this much maligned subject is perhaps testified to by my election to Fellowship in the American Academy of Astrologians, an organization that one can't get into for the asking.

I've wasted enough time playing checkers to have built one of the Egyptian pyramids single-handed. Another hobby is shorthand, which has fascinated me for thirty years. I understand several systems. I can sling a wicked toe on the dance floor, but only dance when my weight crowds two hundred. One year I spent the summer on the desert drying out, where my own

Junius B. Smith

cooking, plus the heat, effected a material reduction. But I come honestly by it: my father weighed two hundred and sixty in athletic condition—three hundred when not.

And speaking of ancestors: My grandfather was a brother of Joseph Smith, who founded the Mormon Church, which probably explains why I was born in Utah.

THE ARGOSY LIBRARY ™

SERIES 6 INCLUDES:

* BRAND * CUMMINGS * BRENT *
FARLEY * AUBREY * ROSCOE *
* GIESY & SMITH *
* LAMB * FOOTNER *
* MCCULLEY *

THE BEST FICTION
FROM THE FRANK
A. MUNSEY LINE

1. GENIUS JONES by Lester Dent
2. WHEN TIGERS ARE HUNTING: THE COMPLETE ADVENTURES OF CORDIE, SOLDIER OF FORTUNE, VOLUME 1 by W. Wirt
3. THE SWORDSMAN OF MARS by Otis Adelbert Kline
4. THE SHERLOCK OF SAGELAND: THE COMPLETE TALES OF SHERIFF HENRY, VOLUME 1 by W.C. Tuttle
5. GONE NORTH by Charles Alden Seltzer
6. THE MASKED MASTER MIND by George F. Worts
7. BALATA by Fred MacIsaac
8. BRETWALDA by Philip Ketchum
9. DRAFT OF ETERNITY by Victor Rousseau
10. FOUR CORNERS, VOLUME 1 by Theodore Roscoe
11. CHAMPION OF LOST CAUSES by Max Brand
12. THE SCARLET BLADE: THE RAKEHELLY ADVENTURES OF CLEVE AND D'ENTREVILLE, VOLUME 1 by Murray R. Montgomery
13. DOAN AND CARSTAIRS: THEIR COMPLETE CASES by Norbert Davis
14. THE KING WHO CAME BACK by Fred MacIsaac
15. BLOOD RITUAL: THE ADVENTURES OF SCARLET AND BRADSHAW, VOLUME 1 by Theodore Roscoe
16. THE CITY OF STOLEN LIVES: THE ADVENTURES OF PETER THE BRAZEN, VOLUME 1 by Loring Brent
17. THE RADIO GUN-RUNNERS by Ralph Milne Farley
18. SABOTAGE by Cleve F. Adams
19. THE COMPLETE CABALISTIC CASES OF SEMI DUAL, THE OCCULT DETECTOR, VOLUME 2: 1912–13 by J.U. Giesy and Junius B. Smith
20. SOUTH OF FIFTY-THREE by Jack Bechdolt

21. TARZAN AND THE JEWELS OF OPAR by Edgar Rice Burroughs

22. CLOVELLY by Max Brand

23. WAR LORD OF MANY SWORDSMEN: THE ADVENTURES OF NORCOSS, VOLUME 1
by W. Wirt

24. ALIAS THE NIGHT WIND by Varick Vanardy

25. THE BLUE FIRE PEARL: THE COMPLETE ADVENTURES OF SINGAPORE SAMMY,
VOLUME 1 by George F. Worts

26. THE MOON POOL & THE CONQUEST OF THE MOON POOL by Abraham Merritt

27. THE GUN-BRAND by James B. Hendryx

28. JAN OF THE JUNGLE by Otis Adelbert Kline

29. MINIONS OF THE MOON by William Grey Beyer

30. DRINK WE DEEP by Arthur Leo Zagat

31. THE VENGEANCE OF THE WAH FU TONG: THE COMPLETE CASES OF JIGGER
MASTERS, VOLUME 1 by Anthony M. Rud

32. THE RUBY OF SURATAN SINGH: THE ADVENTURES OF SCARLET AND
BRADSHAW, VOLUME 2 by Theodore Roscoe

33. THE SHERIFF OF TONTO TOWN: THE COMPLETE TALES OF SHERIFF HENRY,
VOLUME 2 by W.C. Tuttle

34. THE DARKNESS AT WINDON MANOR by Max Brand

35. THE FLYING LEGION by George Allan England

36. THE GOLDEN CAT: THE ADVENTURES OF PETER THE BRAZEN, VOLUME 3
by Loring Brent

37. THE RADIO MENACE by Ralph Milne Farley

38. THE APES OF DEVIL'S ISLAND by John Cunningham

39. THE OPPOSING VENUS: THE COMPLETE CABALISTIC CASES OF SEMI DUAL, THE
OCCULT DETECTOR by J.U. Giesy and Junius B. Smith

40. THE EXPLOITS OF BEAU QUICKSILVER by Florence M. Pettee

41. ERIC OF THE STRONG HEART by Victor Rousseau

42. MURDER ON THE HIGH SEAS AND THE DIAMOND BULLET: THE COMPLETE CASES OF GILLIAN HAZELTINE by George F. Worts

43. THE WOMAN OF THE PYRAMID AND OTHER TALES: THE PERLEY POORE SHEEHAN OMNIBUS, VOLUME 1 by Perley Poore Sheehan

44. A COLUMBUS OF SPACE AND THE MOON METAL: THE GARRETT P. SERVISS OMNIBUS, VOLUME 1 by Garrett P. Serviss

45. THE BLACK TIDE: THE COMPLETE ADVENTURES OF BELLOW BILL WILLIAMS, VOLUME 1 by Ralph R. Perry

46. THE NINE RED GODS DECIDE: THE COMPLETE ADVENTURES OF CORDIE, SOLDIER OF FORTUNE, VOLUME 2 by W. Wirt

47. A GRAVE MUST BE DEEP! by Theodore Roscoe

48. THE AMERICAN by Max Brand

49. THE COMPLETE ADVENTURES OF KOYALA, VOLUME 1 by John Charles Beecham

50. THE CULT MURDERS by Alan Forsyth

51. THE COMPLETE CASES OF THE MONGOOSE by Johnston McCulley

52. THE GIRL AND THE PEOPLE OF THE GOLDEN ATOM by Ray Cummings

53. THE GRAY DRAGON: THE ADVENTURES OF PETER THE BRAZEN, VOLUME 2 by Loring Brent

54. THE GOLDEN CITY by Ralph Milne Farley

55. THE HOUSE OF INVISIBLE BONDAGE: THE COMPLETE CABALISTIC CASES OF SEMI DUAL, THE OCCULT DETECTOR by J.U. Giesy and Junius B. Smith

56. THE SCRAP OF LACE: THE COMPLETE CASES OF MADAME STOREY, VOLUME 1 by Hulbert Footner

57. TOWER OF DEATH: THE ADVENTURES OF SCARLET AND BRADSHAW, VOLUME 3 by Theodore Roscoe

58. THE DEVIL-TREE OF EL DORADO by Frank Aubrey

59. THE FIREBRAND: THE COMPLETE ADVENTURES OF TIZZO, VOLUME 1 by Max Brand

60. MARCHING SANDS AND THE CARAVAN OF THE DEAD: THE HAROLD LAMB OMNIBUS by Harold Lamb